MY BEST FRIEND IS INVISIBLE

ARE YOU BRAVE ENOUGH TO READ THESE Goosebumps?

ALL-NEW! ALL-TERRIFYING!

Goosebumps®

NOW WITH BONUS FEATURES!
LOOK IN THE BACK OF THE BOOK FOR
EXCLUSIVE AUTHOR INTERVIEWS AND MORE.

Night of the Living Dummy
Deep Trouble
Monster Blood
The Haunted Mask
One Day at HorrorLand
(INCLUDES A SECRET GUIDE TO HORRORLAND!)

Goosebumps®

MY BEST FRIEND IS INVISIBLE

R. L. STINE

SCHOLASTIC INC.
New York Toronto London Auckland Sydney
Mexico City New Delhi Hong Kong Buenos Aires

ISBN 0-439-92220-8 (978-0-439-92220-3)

The *Goosebumps* book series created by Parachute Press, Inc.
Published by Scholastic Inc.
SCHOLASTIC, GOOSEBUMPS, and associated logos are trademarks and/or registered trademarks of Scholastic Inc.

12 11 10 9 8 7 6   10 11 12/0

Printed in the U.S.A.   40

MY BEST FRIEND IS INVISIBLE

I sat at the dinner table and wished I was invisible.

If I were invisible, I could sneak away from dinner without finishing my string beans. And I could creep up to my room and finish the book of ghost stories I'd been reading.

I started to daydream. I'm Sammy Jacobs, the Invisible Boy, I told myself. I tried to picture how I'd look if I were invisible.

Last week, I saw a movie about an invisible man. You couldn't see his face or his body. But when he ate, you could see the food digesting in his invisible stomach.

It was totally gross.

I loved it.

Staring at my string beans, I pictured them rolling around in my stomach.

My parents' voices droned on in the background. My parents are research scientists. They work in a college lab. They do weird things with light and lasers.

And then they come home and talk about their work at dinner. And talk about their work. And talk about their work.

My ten-year-old brother, Simon, and I can't get a word in.

We have to sit and listen to them talk about "light refraction" and "ocular impediments."

I'm a science-fiction freak. I love reading science-fiction books and comics. And I rent any movie that has an alien from another planet in it.

But when I have to listen to my parents talk about their work, I feel like an alien from another planet. I mean, I can't understand a single word they say!

"Hey, Mom and Dad." I tried to get into the conversation. "Guess what? I grew a tail today."

Mom and Dad didn't hear me. They were too busy arguing about something called "morphology."

"Actually, I grew *two* tails," I said, louder.

They didn't care. Dad was drawing some kind of chart on his napkin.

I was really bored. I kicked Simon under the table. Just for something to do.

"Ow! Stop it, Sammy!" he cried. He kicked me back.

I kicked him again.

Dad kept scribbling numbers all over his napkin. Mom squinted at his chart.

Simon kicked me back. Too hard.

"Whoa!" I screamed. My hands flew up — and sent my dinner plate flying.

SPLAAT.

Into my lap.

A whole plateful of spaghetti and all the string beans — slid down my jeans.

"Look what Simon made me do!" I shouted.

"You started it!" Simon protested.

Mom glanced up from the chart. At least I had her attention. And maybe I'd even get Simon into trouble. Simon never gets yelled at. He's good.

Mom's gaze shifted from me to Simon. "Simon," Mom started.

All right! I thought. Simon is in for it now!

"Help your clumsy brother clean up," Mom said. She glanced down at the floor and pointed to the pile of spaghetti. "And make sure you mop up this mess." Then she grabbed Dad's pencil and scribbled a bunch of numbers next to his.

Simon tried to help me clean up. But I pushed him away and did it myself.

Was I steamed? Take a guess.

Okay. Okay. Maybe the spaghetti wasn't Simon's fault. But *nothing* is ever Simon's fault. Ever.

Why?

3

I told you — Simon is the good one. He never waits until the last minute to do his homework. He never has to be reminded to throw his clothes in the hamper. Or take out the garbage. Or wipe his feet when he comes in the house.

What kind of kid is that?

A *mutant* — if you ask me.

"Simon is a mutant," I mumbled as I used my napkin to wipe my dinner from my lap.

"My Brother — the Mutant." I smiled. I liked the sound of that. It would make a good science-fiction movie, I decided.

I tossed the paper napkin into the trash and returned to the table.

Well, at least I won't have to eat any more string beans, I thought, staring down at my empty plate.

Wrong.

"Sammy, give me your dish. I'll refill it." Mom stood up, took my plate — and slipped on the spaghetti on the floor.

Uh-oh.

I watched as she lost her balance and slid across the kitchen. I laughed. I couldn't help it. I mean, she looked pretty funny — sliding across the floor like that.

"Who laughed?" Mom turned to face us. "Was it you, Simon?"

"Of course not," Simon answered.

Of course not. Simon's favorite words.

4

Simon — do you want to watch TV? *Of course not.* Want to play ball? *Of course not.* Want to hear a joke? *Of course not.*

Simon would never laugh at Mom.

Simon did only serious things.

Simon — the Serious Mutant.

Mom turned to me and let out a long sigh. She returned to the table with my plate. Refilled. With lots more string beans. Great.

Disappear. Disappear. I stared at my string beans and chanted silently. Last week I read a story about a kid who could make things disappear just by concentrating hard.

It wasn't working for me.

"I can't wait for Saturday to come," I said, burying the string beans under the spaghetti.

"Why?" Simon was the only one who asked.

"I'm going to see *School Spirit*," I told him.

"School spirit?" Dad glanced up from his napkin chart, his eyes finally wide with interest. "School spirit is great! Who has school spirit?"

"Nobody, Dad. *School Spirit* is the name of a new movie. It's about a ghost that haunts an old boarding school," I explained. "I'm going to see it on Saturday."

Dad placed his pencil down. "I wish you were more interested in *real* science, Sammy. I think real science is even stranger than the fantasy stuff you like."

"But ghosts *are* real, Dad!"

5

"Your dad and I are scientists, Sammy," Mom said. "We don't believe in things like ghosts."

"Well, you're wrong," I declared. "If ghosts don't exist, why have there been stories about them for hundreds of years?

"Besides, this movie isn't fantasy stuff," I told them. "It's a true story. Real kids were interviewed for it. Kids who swear they saw the ghost in school!"

Mom shook her head.

Dad chuckled. "What are you doing in school, Simon? Seen any ghosts lately?"

"Of course not," Simon replied. "I'm starting my science project this week. It's called: *How Fast Do We Grow?* I'm going to study myself for six months. And make a growth graph for every part of my body."

"That's wonderful!" Mom said.

"Very original!" Dad exclaimed. "Let us know if we can help."

"Oh, brother," I mumbled, rolling my eyes. "Can I be excused?" I pushed my chair away from the table. "Roxanne is coming over to do math homework."

Roxanne Johnson and I are both in the same seventh-grade class. We like to compete against each other. Just for fun.

At least, I *think* it's for fun. Sometimes I'm not sure what Roxanne thinks.

Anyway, she's one of my best friends. She likes

science fiction too. We planned to see *School Spirit* together.

I went upstairs to search for my math book.

I opened the door to my room.

I stepped inside — and gasped.

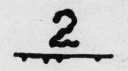

2

My homework papers lay scattered all over the floor.

I'm not exactly the neatest kid in the world — but I do not throw my homework on the floor.

Not usually, anyway.

Well, at least not today.

Brutus — my orange cat — sat in the middle of the mess, with his head buried underneath the pile of papers.

"Brutus — did you do this?" I demanded. Brutus jerked his head up. He glanced at me — then darted under my bed to hide.

Hmmm. That's weird, I thought. Brutus actually looks scared. That is definitely weird.

Brutus never hides from anything. In fact, he's the meanest cat in the neighborhood. Every kid on the block has been scratched by Brutus — at least once.

I looked at the window. It was open. The light-blue curtains billowed in the breeze.

I gathered my papers from the floor. The wind probably blew them off my desk, I guessed.

Wait a minute. Something was wrong.

I stared at the window.

I could *swear* I left that window closed.

But I couldn't have. I mean, there it was — wide-open.

"What are you looking at?" Roxanne stepped into my room.

"Something weird is going on here," I told her, shutting the window. "I closed this before dinner. Now it's open."

"Your mom must have opened it," she said. "What's the big deal, anyway? It's just the window."

"It's no big deal," I said. "But my mom didn't open it. Neither did Dad or Simon. We were all downstairs."

I shook my head. "I *know* I closed it. Brutus was the only one up here — and *he* didn't open it."

I peered under the bed. There was Brutus — snuggled against my sneakers. Shaking.

"Come on, Brutus. Come out," I urged softly. "Don't be afraid. I know she's scary — but it's only Roxanne."

"Very funny, Sammy." Roxanne rolled her eyes. "I'll tell you what's scary. Your brother is scary."

"What do you mean?" I asked.

"I passed him on the way up here. Do you know what he was doing?" she asked.

"No," I said.

"He was lying on the living room floor. On a huge piece of cardboard. Tracing himself," Roxanne replied.

I shrugged. "He must be working on his science project. He's studying himself."

"Your brother is definitely scary," she said. "I'll tell you something else that's scary — the way you ran today. That was very, very scary. I didn't think *anyone* could run that slow!"

Roxanne beat me in the track race at school today. And she wasn't going to let me forget it.

"You won because of only ONE reason," I told her.

"And what was that ONE reason?" she mimicked me.

I slid halfway under the bed and dragged Brutus out. Stalling for time. Stalling so I could come up with a good reason.

"You won because — I let you!" I said finally.

"Yeah, right, Sammy." Roxanne folded her arms across her chest.

"I did. I let you," I insisted.

Roxanne's cheeks turned red. I could see she was getting really steamed.

Making Roxanne angry is fun.

"I let you win — because I wanted to help build up your confidence for the school Olympics," I said.

Whoa! That made Roxanne even angrier. Roxanne doesn't like help from anyone. And she likes to think she's the best at everything.

Our school is going to compete against other schools in a mini-Olympics next week. Roxanne and I are both on the Olympic team. We were both on the team last year too. Roxanne ran every single day to make sure she was the best.

But last year, we lost.

I guess it was my fault. A camera flashed in my face. I tripped — and fell.

"You lost fair and square today, Sammy — and you know it," Roxanne snapped. "And you'd better not trip next week. And make us lose the Olympics again."

"Last year wasn't my fault!" I cried. But Roxanne interrupted me.

"Hey — what's wrong with Brutus?" she asked, peering over my shoulder.

I turned around and saw Brutus sitting in the corner — curled up in a tight ball.

"I don't know. He's acting kind of strange today," I said.

"I know," she agreed. "He didn't even try to scratch me yet. He's been acting — *nice.*"

Brutus stood. He glanced at the window — and arched his back.

Then he turned completely around and sat down, facing the wall.

Weird.

"So? What are we going to do for our term project?" Roxanne asked, plopping down on my bed.

Our term project for our English class was due next month. Ms. Starkling, our teacher, wanted us to work in pairs. She said working in pairs would help us learn about teamwork and cooperation.

"I have a really great idea," I said. "How about a report on plants? You know — how much water they need. Stuff like that."

"That's a really great idea," Roxanne replied. "If you're in kindergarten."

"Okay. Okay. Let me. think." I stood up and paced the room. "Got it! How about the life cycle of a moth? We could catch some — and see how long they take to die!"

Roxanne stared at me. She nodded her head thoughtfully. "I think . . . that's really stupid," she said.

So much for teamwork and cooperation.

"Fine." I folded my arms in front of me. "Why don't *you* try to come up with an idea?"

"I already have," Roxanne declared. "I think we should do a report on *True Haunted Houses*. I know a haunted house right here in Middletown. It's near the woods. Across from the college. I bet we'll find a real ghost living there!"

"There are no haunted houses in Middletown," I said. "I know all about haunted houses — and there isn't one anywhere near here."

12

"The house near the woods *is* haunted," Roxanne insisted. "And that's what we should study for our report. I'll talk to the ghost and take notes. Your job will be to videotape us."

Roxanne never backs down.

Sometimes that's what I like about her.

And sometimes that's what I hate about her. Like now.

"Don't waste your time, Roxanne. I'm practically an expert on ghosts. That house is *not* haunted." I tried to give Roxanne some good advice.

A bad mistake.

"You just don't want to videotape us. You want to be the one who talks to the ghost and takes the notes," she accused.

I let out a sigh.

"But it was my idea — so I get to pick first," Roxanne said. "Ms. Starkling will go crazy when we find a real ghost for our project. We'll probably win an award or something."

"We won't find any ghosts in this town." I shook my head. "This place is too boring. Nothing exciting ever happens here. . . ."

I stopped talking.

A low, frightening moan filled the room.

Roxanne jumped off the bed.

She moved close to me.

We slowly turned toward the sound. Coming from the hall.

13

"Wh-what's that?" Roxanne's voice shook, pointing to the doorway.

We both stared in horror — at an eerie light just outside my room. An eerie white light.

We took a step back.

The light grew brighter.

Closer.

It filled the doorway now.

I held my breath.

"Sammy — *what is it?*" Roxanne's voice quivered.

"I — I don't know."

I watched the strange white light begin to roll and shimmer and stretch — as it reached for us.

We backed up against the wall.

The light grew stronger, whiter.

Blinding now.

Another moan floated toward us — and I gasped.

"A . . . ghost!" I cried. "No. It's a . . . *Dad?*"

Dad stepped into the room. Carrying some sort of bright light.

"That's about as real a ghost as you'll ever find!" Dad laughed.

My heart stopped pounding.

Brutus let out a loud wail and darted from the room.

"Whoa — I didn't think anything could scare that cat!" Dad laughed again.

Mom burst into the room. "You said you were bringing that laser light home to repair it. Not to terrify these kids," she scolded Dad.

"Give me a break. It was just a joke." Dad

turned to us. "You thought it was funny — right, Sammy? Roxanne?"

"Yeah ... very funny, Dad," I said, rolling my eyes. "One of your best jokes. A real riot."

"I knew it was a laser light." Roxanne moved back toward the bed. She sat down, trying to look cool. "When I saw how scared Sammy was, I played along. Super trick, Mr. Jacobs. We really fooled Sammy!"

We really fooled Sammy! *We?*

I wanted to strangle Roxanne.

Sometimes I hate her. HATE her.

Simon wandered into the room, carrying Brutus. "Your stupid cat ran over my body-tracing. He ruined it. Now I have to start all over again."

Simon let Brutus drop to the floor. He glanced at the light Dad held in his hand. Then he looked at me.

"Sammy didn't fall for that dumb light trick — did he?" he asked.

"Why don't you go watch your toes grow!" I shouted at my brother.

"No. This is a different dumb light trick," Dad chuckled.

Mom cleared her throat — a warning to Dad.

"Actually, Simon, this light is called a Molecule Detector Light." Dad tried to turn serious. "Here — have a look at it." He handed the light to Simon.

16

It looked like a regular flashlight — but it definitely wasn't.

A regular flashlight didn't shine with a shimmery, white, blinding light.

"What does it do?" Simon studied the shiny silver casing that housed the laser.

"It's kind of like an X ray," Dad explained. "I can shine it in the air and see all kinds of insects and things that you normally can't see."

"I know what we can use it for." Simon turned the light toward me. "We can use it to find Sammy's BRAIN!"

Everyone laughed. Even Mom.

"Hey! Good one!" Roxanne patted Simon on the back. "That's the first time I ever heard you make a joke."

"I wasn't joking," Simon said flatly.

That made everyone laugh even harder.

"Out!" I yelled. "I want you all to leave!"

Mom, Dad, and Simon left the room. Still laughing.

"What about our math homework?" Roxanne demanded. "I thought we were going to do it together."

"I don't feel like doing it now," I grumbled.

"Okay. Okay." Roxanne backed out of the room. "You don't have to do it. But I do. Ms. Starkling said it's my turn at the chalkboard tomorrow. I want to make sure I get the equations right."

Roxanne left to do her homework.

I opened my math book to do mine.

I stared down at the numbers.

But I couldn't concentrate.

I'll get up early, I decided. And do my homework in the morning.

I got up from my desk to change for bed.

Brutus jumped into my desk chair — his favorite place to sleep.

I crossed the room — and tripped on something in the middle of the floor.

"Hey — what was that?" I spun around.

I glanced at the floor.

"Huh?"

Nothing there.

4

I stared at the floor.

I shook my head.

I tripped over — *nothing?*

It's a good thing Roxanne didn't see this one, I thought. I could hear her making fun of me now. *"Practicing — to make sure we lose the race next week, Sammy?"*

I got into bed.

I propped up my pillows and picked up the ghost-story book I was reading. I stared down at the page, but it was all just a blur.

I closed the book and drifted off to sleep. But I tossed and turned all night long. Half asleep, half awake, I fluffed up my pillow. I pulled the covers up around me. I drifted off again — then woke up to a noise.

Flapping.

The flapping of my curtains in the night breeze.

I sat up. I rubbed my eyes.

I stared at the window.

The *open* window!

I bolted out of bed and slammed it shut.

Who opened this window? WHO?

Is it possible for a window to slide *up*?

NO.

It must be Simon. Simon must be playing a joke on me, I decided.

But it couldn't be Simon. Simon doesn't play jokes. He's always serious.

I climbed back in bed — and stared at the window. Watching. Waiting. Waiting to see it open.

But my eyelids grew heavy and I fell asleep.

The next morning I woke up late. Brutus always wakes me up. But he didn't today.

I bolted up in bed to check the window. Closed.

I glanced at my desk chair. Brutus was gone.

I dressed quickly. I caught my reflection in the mirror as I headed out of my room. I looked wrecked.

"Sammy, you look awful," Mom said. "Did you get to bed late last night?"

I slumped down at the kitchen table. Dad sat across from me, reading the newspaper.

"No, not too late," I told Mom.

Dad peered over the newspaper. "You're reading too many of those ghost books, Sammy. If you read about real science, you'd sleep better."

Dad went back to his newspaper.

Mom poured some cereal into my breakfast bowl. I ate one spoonful — and Simon called me.

"Sammy — come up here," he shouted from his bedroom. "I need your help."

I ignored him.

I ate another spoonful.

"SAM-MY!" he screamed.

"Sammy, go see what your brother wants," Mom ordered.

"SAM-MY! SAM-MY!"

"WHAT?" I cried, charging into his room. "What's your problem?"

"*That!*" he said, pointing to the bed. "That is my problem."

Brutus lay curled up in Simon's bed.

"He slept in here last night," Simon said. "And now I can't get him out. He won't move."

"Brutus slept in here?"

I couldn't believe it.

Brutus always sleeps in my room. Always.

"Yes, he slept in here," Simon said. "And I want him out!"

"What's the big deal? Just leave him there." I turned to the door.

"Wait!" Simon yelled. "I can't leave him there. I can't!"

"Why not?" I asked, confused.

"Because I have to make my bed," Simon answered.

I stared hard at my brother. "What planet are you from?"

"Sammy," Simon whined. "I have to make my bed. Mom says."

"Just make the bed over him. Mom won't notice the lump."

I returned to the kitchen a few seconds later. I sat down at the table.

Mom peered over my shoulder. "Sammy, how did you finish your cereal so fast?"

"Huh?"

I stared down into my breakfast bowl.

Totally empty!

5

"Someone — someone ate my cereal!" I stammered.

"You're right!" Mom gasped. "It must have been a ghost!"

Mom and Dad laughed.

I stared at the empty bowl — and the spoon.

"Look!" I shouted. "Someone *did* eat my cereal. I have proof! The spoon — it's on the left side of the bowl. I always put my spoon on the right side of the bowl — because I'm right-handed. See?"

I pointed to the spoon.

To the proof.

"Stop kidding around, Sammy. You're going to be late for school." Mom turned to Dad. "We'd better get going too."

"Did *you* do it?" I asked Dad as he reached for his briefcase. "Did you eat my cereal? Did you move the spoon? Was it a joke?"

"You're reading too many ghost stories," Dad

said. "Way too many." Then he and Mom hurried off for work.

For a few minutes, I sat at the kitchen table. Just sat there, staring into my empty cereal bowl.

Someone ate my cereal.

I am *not* going crazy, I told myself.

Someone ate my cereal.

But who?

"Sammy. Sammy."

Huh?

"Sammy, would you like to tell us what is so fascinating outside?" Ms. Starkling crossed her arms in front of her, waiting for my answer.

A few kids giggled.

I had been gazing out the classroom window. Thinking — about *my* window. My *open* bedroom window. And my disappearing cereal.

"Uh — no. I mean, nothing," I said. "I mean — I wasn't looking at anything."

Some more giggles.

"Sammy, come up to the chalkboard, please, and show the class how to finish this equation."

"But it's Roxanne's turn," I blurted out. "I mean, isn't Roxanne supposed to show the class today?"

"Sammy, please." Ms. Starkling tapped the chalkboard with a piece of chalk. "Now."

I glanced at Roxanne. She just shrugged her shoulders.

24

I was in big trouble.

I didn't do my math homework last night. And I didn't do it this morning, either — because Brutus didn't wake me up on time.

My temples pounded as I made my way to the front of the classroom. I walked slowly. Staring at the equation. Trying to figure out how to solve it before I got up there.

I had no idea.

Ms. Starkling handed me the piece of chalk.

Silence fell over the classroom.

I stared hard at the numbers on the board.

My palms began to sweat.

"Read the equation out loud," Ms. Starkling suggested. She said it nicely. But I could tell she was losing her patience.

I read the equation out loud.

It didn't help.

I lifted the chalk to the board, even though I still didn't know what to do.

I stared at the numbers some more.

I heard the sounds of kids shifting impatiently in their seats.

I placed the chalk against the board — and gasped.

I felt something squeeze my hand. Something cold and wet.

My knees started to shake.

I felt hot breath right up against my face.

I tried to step back — but I couldn't move.

Something squeezed my fingers tighter and tighter. Squeezed until it hurt.

The breathing against my face grew more rapid — sharp gasps that stung my cheeks.

I wanted to pull free. But then my hand started to move across the chalkboard.

My hand was moving — and it started to write!

Someone was writing numbers for me! Someone was holding my hand! Moving it! Solving the equation!

Someone I couldn't see!

6

I yanked my hand back. I jerked free of the clammy, invisible grip.

Then I dropped the chalk — and started screaming.

And ran from the room.

I ran into the hall. I leaned against the wall outside the classroom. My hands were shaking. My knees trembled.

I could still feel the cold, ghostly fingers wrapped around my hand.

I heard Roxanne inside — volunteering to finish the equation.

"Sammy." Ms. Starkling met me out in the hall. "What happened? Are you sick? Would you like to see the school nurse?"

"I'm — I'm not sick," I stammered.

I didn't want to explain what happened.

I couldn't explain it. I didn't even want to try.

"Are you sure you don't want to see the nurse?

You don't look well." Ms. Starkling felt my forehead.

"No. I'm okay," I lied. "I — I just felt a little dizzy — because I didn't eat breakfast this morning."

Ms. Starkling believed me. She sent me to the lunchroom to get something to eat.

As I made my way down the hall, I could still feel the clammy hand gripping my fingers.

Still feel the hot breath on my face.

Still feel the cold force as it pushed my hand along the board. Guiding it. Writing the numbers for me.

I shivered.

Maybe Dad is right. Maybe I *have* been reading too many ghost stories.

I walked home alone after school. I wanted to be by myself. To think.

I heard footsteps behind me. Footsteps pounding the pavement. Running toward me.

"Sammy — wait up!" It was Roxanne.

I pretended I didn't hear her. I kept walking.

"Sammy!" Roxanne caught up — out of breath. "What happened to you today?"

"Nothing happened."

"Something happened," she insisted. "Something happened to you in math class."

"I don't want to talk about it," I told her.

"I'm really good at math," Roxanne said smugly. "I'd be happy to help you — if you don't understand it."

"I . . . don't . . . need . . . help," I replied through gritted teeth. I began to walk faster — but Roxanne kept up with me.

We didn't talk.

Finally, Roxanne broke the silence. "Let's go to the haunted house Saturday night. For our project. Okay?"

"Maybe. I have to get home now. I'll call you later to talk about it."

I broke into a run — and left Roxanne on the sidewalk, staring after me.

I wanted to get home.

I wanted to think about everything that had happened.

I wanted to think about it — by myself.

As I headed into the house, I wondered about my bedroom window. Would it be open? I made sure it was closed before I left this morning. But that didn't mean anything.

I started up the stairs. But I stopped when I heard Brutus meowing loudly in the kitchen. He always does that when he wants to go out.

"Okay. Okay. I'm coming."

Brutus started to wail.

"Hold it down, Brutus. I said I was —"

I stopped in the kitchen door.

There was Brutus — crouched on a chair. His fur stood straight up. He pulled back his lips in a menacing hiss.

I followed his gaze — and let out a shriek.

A pizza sat on the table.

A slice from the pie floated above the plate — floated up by itself.

I stared in shock as it rose higher and higher.

"Who — who's there?" I stammered. "I know someone is there! Who ARE you?"

7

"Who are you?" I demanded again.

No answer.

I stared at the pizza slice. Stared as it floated in midair.

I watched as it was chewed up. Bite by bite.

"Tell me who you are!" I shouted. "You're really scaring me!"

Another bite disappeared from the floating slice of pizza. And another.

"This isn't happening. It can't be," I whispered.

I'll close my eyes. When I open them — I'll see that I imagined the whole thing, I told myself.

And I'll never read a ghost book again, I promised.

Or watch a sci-fi movie.

Another bite of the pizza disappeared.

I closed my eyes.

I opened them.

The slice of pizza was gone.

I let out a long sigh of relief.

Then I realized it was gone — EATEN.

"WHO ARE YOU?" I demanded. "Tell me — right now. Or I'll —"

"Sammy — who are you talking to?" Mom stood in the kitchen doorway, staring at me.

"There's someone here!" I cried. "Someone eating pizza!"

"I can see that!" Mom said. "I can see that someone has eaten half a pizza — before dinner. Sammy, you know you're not supposed to eat before dinner!"

"I didn't! It wasn't me!" I cried.

"Of course it wasn't you," Mom said. "It was the ghost from this morning — right? The one who ate your cereal. Sammy, please. This is serious. How many times have I told you — no snacking before dinner. You're old enough to know better!"

"But, Mom —"

"No buts! I want you to go up to your room and straighten it up before we eat," Mom ordered. "You left it a mess this morning. Please put your dirty clothes in the hamper and make your bed."

"But half the day is over. It doesn't make sense to make my bed now," I argued.

"Sam-my!" Mom narrowed her eyes. Mom narrows her eyes when she's angry. Right now her eyes were really narrowed. "GO!"

Mom opened the refrigerator to get a drink.

I turned to leave the kitchen — and froze.

Right behind Mom, Brutus started to rise up

from the kitchen chair. Floating up. Rising higher and higher.

His fur stood straight up. He gazed down at the floor and let out a cry. He stretched out his paws to leap —

"Mom, look!" I cried. "Look at Brutus!"

Mom whirled around — too late. Brutus had landed safely back on the kitchen chair.

Mom's eyes grew really, really narrow. "Go up to your room now, Sammy!"

What could I do?

I left the kitchen and headed for the stairs. I turned into my room — and gasped.

My room!

My room looked like a garbage dump.

Cereal boxes were strewn on the bed. Greasy food containers and crushed juice boxes littered my desk, my dresser, my chair — everywhere.

I took a step inside and heard a loud crunch. I glanced down — and groaned. Frosted Flakes and Corn Pops carpeted the floor.

"Who did this?" I cried. "WHO TRASHED MY ROOM?"

I collapsed on my bed — and felt something sticky on the back of my pants. "Oooh, gross!" I moaned. "Peanut butter and jelly."

I pulled back the blanket for a clean place to sit — and found strands of last night's spaghetti and some half-eaten chicken legs.

"Who would do this?" I shook my head. "WHO?"

Does Simon's room look like this? I wondered. And Mom and Dad's room? I ran down the hall to check.

Simon's room was spotless. Mom and Dad's room was perfectly clean too.

I walked back to my room — and froze.

"Sammy!" Mom planted her hands firmly on her hips. Her face burned red with anger. "What have you done?"

8

"I — I didn't do it, Mom!" I cried. "I didn't make this mess!"

"Give me a break," Mom sighed. "If you didn't do it, who did? I didn't do it! Your father didn't do it! Simon didn't do it! Tell me, Sammy — who did it?"

"M-maybe it *was* Simon." I didn't know what else to say. But I shouldn't have said that.

"First you trash your room. Then you try to blame your little brother! Sammy — I don't know what's gotten into you! I don't want to see you downstairs until this room sparkles. Your father and I will discuss what to do about you later."

Mom turned to leave. "And don't come down for dinner. You've eaten quite enough!"

I stood in the center of my room and listened to Mom's footsteps fade down the stairs.

"How am I going to clean this mess?" I moaned. "It will take me a year."

"I'll help you."

Who said that?

I spun around to face the doorway.

No one there.

"Come on, Sammy," a boy's voice urged. "Let's get going, or we'll never clean up this mess."

I watched in disbelief as a cereal box floated up from my bed. Floated up and threw itself into the trash.

"Who — who are you?" I stammered. "How do you know my name?"

Another cereal box started to rise. And another. They tossed themselves into the trash too.

I waited for the boy to answer me.

But he didn't.

I stared at the last cereal box — waiting for it to rise up.

It didn't move.

"Where are you?" I whispered.

No answer.

I scanned my bedroom — searching for a sign of him. *Where did he go?*

I heard a rustling sound and spun around.

My pillow hovered in the air. I watched as the pillowcase slid off it — all by itself!

"Where are the clean sheets, Sammy? You know, you should make your bed in the morning — like Simon."

"How do you know me?" My voice started to rise. "How do you know my name? Who *are* you?"

"Calm down," the boy said. "No reason to get

stressed. I arrived last night. I found out your name from Roxanne."

"You — you know Roxanne?" I sputtered.

"No. I don't know Roxanne. I heard her use your name last night," he explained. "When she came over to do homework with you."

"*What* . . . are . . . you?" I asked slowly.

My heart pounded as I waited for the boy's answer. But he didn't answer me.

"WHAT ARE YOU?" I cried out. "Tell me! WHAT ARE YOU? Are you a . . . GHOST?"

9

"A ghost!" The boy broke into a fit of laughter.

"You don't believe in ghosts — do you?" the boy asked.

"No, of course not," I shouted. "I don't believe in ghosts. I just believe in invisible kids!"

"Okay. Okay. I see your point," he said. "No — I'm not a ghost. I'm alive."

A loud, scraping sound cut through the air.

I jumped in surprise — and saw my chair move out from my desk.

"I hope it's okay if I sit down," he said. "Wow — is it hot in here." Yesterday's math homework floated up from my desk and began fanning the air.

"Are you the one who keeps opening my bedroom window?" I demanded.

"Uh-huh. It's really hot up here. Why do you keep it so hot in your room?" he asked.

"Forget about the window!" I said. "What do you want? Why are you here? Did you trash my room?"

"Uh . . . I guess I really made a mess in here. I was really hungry. Sorry. But I'll help you clean up." The boy's voice grew softer. "I just want to be your friend, Sammy."

"That's ridiculous!" I said. "How can you be my friend? I can't even see you! You're invisible!"

"I know," the boy said softly. He sounded kind of sad. "I've been invisible for as long as I can remember. That's why it's so hard to have friends."

"Well — where are your parents?" I asked.

"I don't know. I really don't. My parents left me here for some reason. I don't know where they went. I know my name. That's about it. My name is Brent Green, and I'm twelve."

Brent Green. An invisible boy. Right in my room.

It was hard to believe.

I mean, I've read a ton of science-fiction books. And I really believe in a lot of that stuff. But an invisible boy right in my room. Whoa!

"Brent, I don't know if I can be friends with you. I mean — this is weird."

"Sammy, who are you talking to?" Simon walked into my room. He glanced around. "Hey! There's no one here. Were you talking to yourself?"

I turned away from my desk chair. "Yeah, Simon. I was talking to myself."

I didn't want to tell Simon about Brent. Not yet anyway. I wanted to find out more about him first.

I wanted to be an expert on invisible people before I told anyone in my family!

"You're nuts, Sammy. You're really nuts." Simon gazed around the room. "Boy, this place is a total mess. How could you do this? No wonder Mom is so angry. You are in major trouble. Major trouble."

Simon picked up a chicken bone from my bed. "Yuck!" He held it between two fingers, then let it drop back on the sheet. "That's gross!"

He tiptoed carefully over the cereal on the floor.

He slowly made his way to my chair. Brent's chair.

"Don't sit there —" I tried to warn Simon.

But it was too late.

I watched as the chair flew out from under Simon. Flew out — all by itself.

Simon landed hard on the floor! He sat in a glob of grape jelly, his mouth gaping open in shock.

"That was mean, Sammy! I'm telling Mom!"

"I didn't do anything!" I protested. "You missed the chair. It was your own fault!"

Simon struggled to his feet and marched out of my room.

"Ha! Ha!" Brent laughed. "Good one! Right, Sammy? I pulled the chair right out from under him!"

Simon was downstairs right now — telling Mom what a horrible thing I had done to him. But I was already in trouble, I decided. So what difference did it make? And I had to admit it — watching Simon fall was pretty funny.

Maybe having an invisible friend wouldn't be too weird after all. I mean — it could be kind of fun.

"Brent — what is it like to be invisible? I mean — can you walk through things?" I asked.

"No," Brent answered. "I can't walk *through* anything."

"Are you . . . uh . . . dressed?" I asked.

Brent laughed. "Don't worry, Sammy. I'm dressed," he said. Then he sighed loudly. "You know, I'm just a regular kid. I'm just like you — only invisible."

I'm just like you — only invisible.

Suddenly I had a great idea.

"Brent, could you make me invisible? Just for a little while. So I could see what it's like?"

"I wish I could. That would be fun. But I don't know how to make someone invisible. Sorry," he apologized. "Hey! I think we'd better get back to work here. This place is still a disaster."

Brent and I finished cleaning the room just as the front doorbell rang.

I heard Mom answer it. A second later Roxanne burst into my room, carrying about a thousand books. She let them drop to the floor with a crash.

"Hi, Sammy." She smiled. "I came over to help you with your homework. I brought all my math books."

"Boy, am I glad you're here!" I said.

Roxanne smiled. "I knew you'd want my help."

"Not with that." I shoved her books aside. "I want you to meet someone. His name is Brent —

and he's an invisible boy. And he's here! Right in this room!"

Roxanne's eyes opened wide. "An invisible boy?" she whispered.

"Yes!" I said. "He's here!"

Roxanne glanced around my room — and screamed. "I — I see him!"

"You DO?" I asked.

"Yes!" she repeated, pointing to my desk. "I see him. He's standing right there!"

11

"You can *see* him?" I gasped, amazed.

I faced my desk.

I squinted.

Stared really hard.

I didn't see a thing.

Roxanne laughed. "Gotcha!"

She gave me a not-so-friendly clap on the back, and I stumbled forward. "I'm tired of this dumb game." Roxanne groaned. "Do you want to do math or not?"

"But — I'm not kidding," I insisted. "This is not a joke."

Roxanne dropped down on my bed and sighed.

"I'll prove it to you," I told her. "Watch."

I gazed around my room, trying to figure out where he was. "Brent — pick up one of Roxanne's books from the floor," I said. "Show her you're here."

I lowered my gaze to the floor. Wait till she sees this! I thought. She'll totally freak!

I kept my eyes glued to the pile. Waiting for one of them to float up.

Nothing happened.

"PLEASE, Brent," I begged.

I grabbed a pencil from my desk. I held it out. "Take this pencil from me. Make it float across the room!"

Nothing.

Roxanne rolled her eyes. "Please! I don't have time for these stupid jokes, Sammy. Besides, it's not funny."

"Brent? Hey — Brent?"

It was no use. Brent was not going to cooperate.

I dropped into my desk chair and threw my hands up into the air. "Thanks, Brent. Thanks a lot."

"Ready for math?" Roxanne asked.

"No. I'm not ready," I snapped.

"You don't have to yell," she said. "Actually — I came over for another reason." She slid off the bed and started collecting her math books from the floor.

"I came over to see if we're going to the haunted house Saturday night or not."

"We don't have to go to the haunted house," I cried. "We can do our report right here. Right in my room. We can do our report on Brent. Brent — The Invisible Kid!"

"Yeah. Yeah. Yeah." Roxanne started to lift her big pile of books from the floor. "The Invisible Kid. Right."

My shoulders sagged.

"Listen, Sammy. We have to start our project. It's going to be the best report in the whole class. No — it will be the best report anyone ever did in the history of the whole school."

"Can't we talk about this tomorrow, Roxanne? I'm really not in the mood right now."

I was tired — and hungry. I hadn't eaten anything since lunchtime. And I wanted to try to talk to Brent again.

"No! We cannot talk about this tomorrow!" I could see that Roxanne was beginning to lose her patience. "We have to start planning now. I want to go to Hedge House Saturday night."

"What's Hedge House?" I asked.

Roxanne sighed loudly. "Hedge House is *the* haunted house. The one near the college. That's what it's called. I've been reading all about it."

Roxanne shuffled through her pile of books. "Here it is! Here's the book about Hedge House. Do you want to hear some of it?"

Do I have a choice? I asked myself. I leaned back in my chair and tried to pay attention.

Roxanne stood in the middle of the room and began to read.

"There have been many stories about the horrors of Hedge House," she started. "But the true horror began when the Stilson family moved into town. They moved into Hedge House. No one had lived there in years — because everyone knew the house was haunted.

"Tall, dark hedges grew around the house, enclosing it, sealing it off from curious eyes.

"Every year, the hedges grew taller and darker, until they turned the color of night and shaded the highest windows.

"The local people knew why the hedges grew that way. 'It's the will of the ghost,' they'd say. 'To keep the house chilly and dark — as cold and icy as the spirit itself.'

"Everyone knew that — everyone but the Stilson family.

"From the day the Stilsons moved in, the Hedge House ghost visited ten-year-old Jeffrey Stilson's bedroom. The ghost visited every night.

"'*Jef-frey*,' the ghost moaned. '*Jef-frey — I've been waiting for you.*'

"Each night, Jeffrey woke up shaking, frightened. He stared hard into the darkness of his room, searching for the man behind the voice. But no one was ever there.

"He told his parents about the nightly visits. Told them again and again.

"But they didn't believe him.

"'*Jef-frey, I've been waiting for you*,' the ghost's voice returned one very chilly evening. '*I need you.*'

"'What do you want?' Jeffrey cried out. 'Tell me what you want —'

"At the sound of Jeffrey's voice, the ghost appeared.

"It was the ghost of a young man. From a time long ago. Jeffrey could tell, from the clothes it wore — short, baggy black pants that ended below the knees. Black socks pulled up high to meet the pants cuffs. And black boots with shiny silver buckles.

"Jeffrey stared at the ghost.

"He stared in horror at its black shirt. At the right sleeve that hung loosely at the ghost's side. The sleeve with no arm inside.

"*'Come with me, Jeffrey,*' the ghost moaned. *'Come with me — to learn the secret of this awful house.'*"

Roxanne closed the book and placed it down on the bed.

"What's the secret?" I demanded. "What's the secret of Hedge House?"

"I don't know. I haven't gotten to that part yet," Roxanne said. "But I can tell you this. I know some people who've been inside Hedge House. And they say all kinds of spooky things happen there."

"Like what?" I asked.

"Well, they say the doors open and close all by themselves," she replied.

I gasped — as the door behind Roxanne opened and closed by itself.

"That's right, Sammy," Roxanne said. "It *does*

make you lose your breath when you think about it."

The door opened and closed again.

Very funny, Brent! I thought.

"And they say the books float right off the bookshelves," Roxanne continued.

Brent began juggling three of my schoolbooks behind Roxanne's back. Round and round they went, with the middle one always popping up — right over Roxanne's head!

I couldn't help myself. I started to laugh.

"What's so funny, Sammy?" Roxanne frowned at me.

I raised my hand to point behind her. But the books floated back to the shelf.

I sighed. "Nothing."

"Good. Because this is *not* funny. I'm very serious about this report. I want it to be the best. And I want you to take great video shots to prove the ghost of Hedge House really exists!"

My video camera floated up from the floor, aimed itself at Roxanne's back — and I burst out laughing again.

"SAMMY!" Roxanne jumped up angrily. "Quit it!" she shouted. "I'm going to strangle you if you don't stop laughing! This report means a lot to me. It's not just the grade. If I really do find the ghost, it's going to make me famous!"

"Huh?" I stared at her.

Roxanne took a deep breath. Then she continued. "They say the ghost really hates light. They say if a light shines on him, he explodes into a rage — and destroys anything that is in his path."

I heard a soft squeak.

I glanced around the room — and saw the lightbulb in the ceiling fixture turning. Turning all by itself.

Brent is standing on my dresser, I realized. He's unscrewing the lightbulb!

"Roxanne, quick!" I shouted. "Look up at the ceiling! See that? Now do you believe me!"

12

"Do you see it, Roxanne?" I jumped up from my chair — really excited. Now Roxanne would *have* to believe me!

I pointed to the lightbulb as it slowly turned in the socket — by itself!

"See!" I shouted. Now you believe me — right? It's the invisible kid!"

I spun around. I couldn't wait to see the amazed look on her face!

Roxanne wasn't amazed.

In fact, I couldn't even see her face.

She was kneeling down, head bent, gathering her books up from the floor.

I glanced back up at the ceiling. The lightbulb wasn't turning anymore.

"Roxanne! Why didn't you look?" I cried. "You missed it! You should have looked when I told you to!"

"I should have picked a different partner," Roxanne groaned. "I'm tired of your dumb jokes, Sammy!"

I collapsed back into my desk chair.

Roxanne balanced the stack of books in her arms and headed for the door. "Oh, I get it!" She whirled around to face me. "Now I understand what you're doing."

"Huh?"

"If you don't want to come with me to the haunted house — just say so!" Roxanne said. "You don't have to make up these stupid stories."

Roxanne was angry.

I usually enjoy making Roxanne angry. But not this time.

"An idiot," she mumbled under her breath. "You must think I'm a total idiot. I'm leaving now, Sammy. I'm leaving you — *and* your invisible friend!"

Then she stormed out of my room.

"Are you still here, Brent?" I asked, searching around.

No answer.

I jumped up from my chair.

"I know you're here, Brent. Why did you do that to me?" I clenched my fists into two tight balls. "Why didn't you show Roxanne that you were here?" I cried angrily.

Silence.

"Okay. Okay. I'm sorry I yelled. I didn't really

mean to yell at you, Brent. I just wanted Roxanne to believe me."

I sat back down in my chair.

I took a deep breath.

"Did you hear me, Brent? I said I was sorry."

No answer.

"Please answer me," I pleaded. "I want to talk to you. I want to find out more about you!"

The room remained silent.

Brent was gone.

For good?

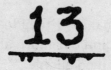

13

Did Brent really leave?

Did he leave because I yelled at him? I wondered.

Would he come back?

I was still asking myself these questions on the way to school the next morning.

An invisible kid.

An invisible kid was in my room yesterday.

Whoa!

This was hard to believe.

I wanted to tell Mom and Dad about Brent last night. But I wasn't allowed out of my room. Even after I had cleaned it up.

That was Simon's fault. He told them I made him fall. So Mom and Dad ordered me to stay in my room all night — and think about how lucky I was to have a younger brother.

That took about a second.

The rest of the night I thought about Brent.

What did he really want? I wondered, as the

school bus rumbled toward school. He says he wants a friend. But should I believe him?

I mean — a kid shows up in your room. An *invisible* kid. That's pretty weird right there. And then he says he *just* wants to be your friend.

Suddenly, I had a bad feeling about him.

He wants something from me. I just know it. I've read tons of books about ghosts . . . monsters . . . you name it.

And I can tell you this. They *always* want something. Your body. Your brain. Your blood. Something.

My body. That's it.

That has to be it.

Brent is a ghost who wants to fool me into being his friend — so he can take over my body!

The thought made me shudder.

Last night, I'd been too shocked — too amazed — to be frightened of him. But now, I had time to think. And I was really getting scared.

Why did he come to our house? To my room?

Maybe I can make a deal with him, I thought. *Leave me alone — and I'll give you my brother!*

I knew Brent wouldn't go for that one — but it made me smile.

I didn't smile for long, though.

I walked into school and stopped inside the doorway. I saw Claire, a girl from my class, standing by the water fountain.

"Sure. I'll go with you after school," I heard her say. "Don't worry — I'll be there."

My mouth dropped open.

Claire was talking — to *no one*.

I walked slowly to my locker.

A boy I knew from art class struggled with his lock. "Why can't I get this thing open?" he complained. "It never got stuck before."

He turned to his left and said, "Okay — you do it."

And there was no kid standing next to him.

He was also talking to someone invisible!

I stared down the long hall.

It was filled with kids. Kids talking. Kids talking to invisible kids!

The school is filled with them! I realized to my horror.

The school is filled with invisible people!

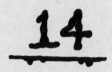

14

"Sammy!"

I turned to see who called my name — praying I *could* see who it was.

I sighed with relief.

It was Roxanne.

"Roxanne! You're not going to believe —" I started. Then I stopped.

Roxanne was grinning.

She walked up to me and laughed right in my face.

All the other kids in the hall began to laugh too.

"You — you *told* everyone?" I sputtered. "You told everyone about the invisible kid in my room?"

Roxanne tried to speak, but she couldn't. She was doubled over, laughing really hard now. She nodded yes.

"How could you do this to me?" I screeched.

"Calm down." Roxanne patted me on the shoulder. "It was just a joke. You have to admit we all did a good job of keeping a straight face."

"Ha ha," I said weakly. I didn't think it was the least bit funny. *I'm going to get Roxanne for this*, I promised myself. *I don't know how — but I will.*

I headed into my classroom with my head down and took my seat quickly.

The other kids piled into the room. Some of them were still laughing. When they saw me, they pretended to talk to invisible people again.

My face turned red.

"Everyone is so chatty this morning!" Ms. Starkling noted. "Time to settle down. Please take out your homework."

"Oh, no," I groaned.

I didn't do my homework last night. I'd forgotten all about it.

I glanced around the room.

I was the only one without the assignment.

"Please pass your homework to the front of the room," Ms. Starkling said.

Claire sat in front of me. She waited for me to pass my homework to her before she passed hers up.

I tapped her on the shoulder. "I don't have it," I whispered.

"Uh-oh," she said. "Did the invisible boy eat it?" Everyone around me giggled.

"Quiet down, class," Ms. Starkling warned. She collected all the homework, then told us to open our math books.

Ms. Starkling wrote an equation on the board. "Sammy, are you feeling better today?" she asked when she finished.

I nodded yes.

I mean — what else could I say? *No. Ms. Starkling, I'm not feeling better. I met an invisible kid last night in my room — and now no one will ever believe me. Everyone thinks I'm crazy.*

"Good," Ms. Starkling said. "Would you please come up and show the class how to solve this?"

I couldn't catch a break today.

I stood up.

"Not you, Sammy," Ms. Starkling said. "I was talking to him."

She pointed to the seat next to me.

The empty seat next to me.

I glanced up at Ms. Starkling, puzzled.

"Your invisible friend," she said.

That sent the whole class into a new fit of laughter.

Ms. Starkling laughed. "Sorry, Sammy. I had to get in on the joke too."

Sorry? I knew she wasn't sorry. She was laughing too hard.

I was so embarrassed. Totally humiliated.

And that was just the beginning of the day. The afternoon was much worse.

At lunch period, I went to the library. I took a seat by myself.

I didn't want to hear any more invisible boy jokes.

I didn't want to talk to anyone.

I took my tuna sandwich out of my backpack. I placed it on my lap so Ms. Pinsky, the librarian, wouldn't see it. We're not supposed to eat in the library, and I didn't want to get caught.

Everyone in school knows that when the librarian gets angry — watch out. I remember when Claire made her angry. Ms. Pinsky made Claire write a hundred book reports, three pages each! That was last year — but Claire is still writing the reports. I think she's only up to book number twenty.

I unwrapped the sandwich — and gasped.

The sandwich began to rise up.

"Brent — put it down!" I whispered. "What are you doing here?"

A bite disappeared from the sandwich.

"I was lonely in your room, all by myself," Brent said. "And hungry." Another bite of my sandwich vanished.

I snatched the sandwich away from him. I glanced nervously around the room. "You can't stay here. You have to leave!"

"Please, let me stay," Brent begged. "It's no fun at home without you. I need a friend."

"Everyone thinks I'm nuts!" My voice started to rise. "Totally NUTS! All the kids in school are laughing at me. Even my teacher is making fun of me! You can't stay here, Brent. You can't —"

A shadow fell over the table.

I glanced up.

The librarian stood over me, frowning and shaking her head.

15

"Ssssammy!" she hissed. "Who are you talking to? And why are you talking in the library?"

I gulped.

Her eyes narrowed into two angry slits. She clenched her lips tightly together.

Then she glanced down at my lap and gasped. "Is that . . . FOOD?"

I'm doomed, I realized. I'll be writing book reports for the rest of my life. Thanks, Brent. Thanks a lot.

"Sammy! How could you?" the librarian exclaimed. "You've broken my two most important rules!"

I grabbed onto my seat, waiting for her to really let me have it. But she didn't.

"This is so unlike you," she said. Her voice grew kinder. "Would you like to talk to the guidance counselor after school today? You know, talking to yourself is a sign that you are troubled by something."

I glanced around the library — at everyone gaping at me. I could feel my face turning hot. I knew I was blushing.

"No, I'm fine," I insisted.

"If something is bothering you — it's nothing to be ashamed of." The librarian took a seat next to me.

Now everyone started to whisper.

I wanted to disappear.

"Nothing is troubling me. Really," I insisted, shoving my sandwich back in my backpack.

"Maybe you should have a chat with the guidance counselor anyway," she continued. "I'm sure you'll find Ms. Turnbull very easy to talk to. I'll tell her you are going to stop by."

The librarian was not going to give up.

"I can't see Ms. Turnbull after school today. I'm in the relay race in the Olympics," I said. "I can't miss the race. My whole team is depending on me!"

"Okay." The librarian stood up to leave. "But will you promise me something?"

Sure, I thought. I'll promise you anything — as long as you leave. NOW.

I nodded yes.

"I want you to come and see me if anything is bothering you. Will you do that?" She patted me on the shoulder.

I nodded again — and she went back to her desk.

I slowly glanced around — to see if everyone was still staring at me.

They weren't.

They were all busy talking. Talking to invisible friends. And laughing.

I shaded my eyes from the sun. It beamed down brightly on the track field.

The sky was a deep blue.

The air felt warm. Nice. Not too hot.

A perfect day for a race.

I peered into the bleachers. They spilled over with kids from all the schools in town.

More kids arrived, trying to push their way into seats. But the bleachers were packed. Kids shouted and shoved and laughed and joked. Everyone seemed totally wired.

My team gathered at one end of the field. I jogged over to them.

"Hey! Sammy!" Roxanne greeted me and slapped me a high five. "Great day for a race! I know we're going to win — I can feel it!" And then she added, "Unless you mess up."

"You don't have to worry about me, Roxanne. I can outrun *you* any day," I shot back.

I ran a practice lap around the field. I ran fast and strong. I was pumped up. I felt totally confident.

Three of us were going to run the relay race.

Jed would start. Jed is a great runner. He's tall and skinny and can take really long strides.

I would run next. Then Roxanne would finish up.

The three of us were the fastest runners in the whole seventh grade.

We couldn't lose.

The race was about to begin. I jumped up and down to keep my muscles warm.

I glanced up into the stands — and saw some kids pointing at me. Some of them laughed.

"Oh, noooo," I moaned. I know what they're talking about. My invisible friend.

After this race, you are going to keep a promise you made this morning, I told myself. You are going to pay Roxanne back — no matter what it takes.

All my muscles tensed up.

"Relax. Relax," I repeated over and over, bending forward and rubbing my leg muscles.

"Ready, Sammy?" Jed high-fived me. "We're counting on you!"

"Ready!" I said.

But I couldn't stop thinking about the kids in the bleachers — the ones who laughed every time they looked at me.

And I couldn't stop thinking about Ms. Starkling — and how she made fun of me.

And I couldn't stop thinking about the librarian — who thought I was totally nuts.

My muscles tightened even more.

I concentrated hard. Concentrated on shoving all those thoughts out of my mind.

I did some warm-up exercises. My muscles began to loosen up. I started to feel better.

The referee took his place on the field.

Jed, Roxanne, and I lined up in race order.

The six teams from the other schools were ready too. We all waited for the referee's signal. As soon as he blew his whistle, the first runner would run around the track once — then pass the baton to the next runner.

I trained my eyes on the referee. My heart pounded. I took a deep breath. Then another.

The whistle blew.

The race was on!

Cheers rang out as Jed took off! He ran faster than I'd ever seen him run before. Amazing!

Roxanne and I cheered him on. "Go, Jed! Gooooo!"

Jed reached the halfway mark before any of the other runners.

He raced to the finish. Practically flying now. Holding out the baton. Holding it out so I could grab it — and run.

I could hear his sneakers pounding the ground. Dust flew up behind him. His face was red. His eyes were wide.

He was only a few feet away from me.

I dropped into my racing position.

I stuck out my hand.

Jed stretched out his arm.

I grabbed the baton from him. The cheers in the bleachers rose to a roar.

Here I go! I thought. *RUN!*

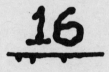

16

My shoes pounded the track. I swung my arms hard, gripping the baton in my right hand.

I took long strides, leaning forward, building a rhythm. Faster. Faster than I'd ever run.

The cheers thundered in my ears. "Go, Sammy! Go! Go! Go!"

That made me run even harder.

It felt so awesome!

Without slowing down, I glanced over my shoulder.

I was way ahead of all the other runners.

I reached the halfway mark — and sprinted forward. We were going to win this race! *Yes!*

The three-quarter mark was coming up — and I wasn't even out of breath. The other runners were struggling, still way behind.

I leaned forward. Pounded the hard track.

And gasped when I felt a hand grab my shoulder.

Another hand grabbed my waist.

"Hey — !" I cried.

And then I realized what was happening.

"Brent — get away! What are you doing?" I wailed.

"I'm going to help you win!" he cried breathlessly. "I'm going to show you I'm your friend! Watch!"

Before I knew what was happening —

Before I could stop him —

My feet lifted up off the ground — and I started to fly!

17

"No! Stop! Put me down! *Put me down!*" I shrieked.

He ignored my cries. He raised me off the ground.

I flew about a foot. And felt Brent stumble.

"Let go! Let go!" I screamed.

I waved my arms wildly, trying to regain my balance. I kicked my legs, trying to break free of Brent's grasp.

I let out an angry cry as I fell to the track.

I landed hard on my knees and elbows. Then my head banged down on the sharp cinders.

The baton flew from my hand. I gazed up — and watched in horror as it rolled across the field.

"Ohhhhh."

"Sorry, Sammy," Brent cried from close by. "I only wanted to help. But I tripped."

I looked up — in time to see the other runners racing by me.

We were going to lose. Big time.

I raised my eyes to Roxanne and Jed. They glared back at me. They shook their fists angrily at me.

I sat up. My elbows were scraped raw. My knees were bleeding.

"Brent! How could you do this to me?" I wailed.

"I was only trying to help," he repeated.

Another runner raced by me. His sneakers kicked up a chunk of cinders and mud. *SPLAT* — into my eyes.

I felt a hand trying to wipe the mud away.

I swung out my arm and shoved Brent hard.

"Ow!" he cried. "Hey — why do you have to be a sore loser? Winning isn't everything, you know."

With my head down, I shuffled off the field. As I walked by the bleachers, some kids from my school booed me.

I got some cheers too — mostly from kids on the other teams.

I could feel Jed's and Roxanne's burning glares as I made my way over to them.

Jed didn't say a word. I think he was too angry to speak.

Roxanne didn't have that problem.

"How *could* you — you stupid clumsy cretin!" she shrieked. "We could have won! You blew it. You really blew it this time!"

"It wasn't my fault!" I cried. "It was the invisible kid!"

Ugh. Wrong thing to say.

"I wish *you* were invisible!" Roxanne cried in disgust.

I wish I were invisible too, I thought. This has to be the most awful day of my life.

Brent is ruining my life.

Maybe having an invisible friend would be fun for another kid. But it was definitely not fun for me.

I have to do something about Brent, I decided.

I have to do something right away.

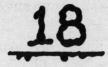

18

"Come on, Sammy. Be a good sport. Measure me." Simon shoved a tape measure in my face.

"I told you, Simon. You haven't grown since yesterday! Now — leave me alone."

I had just returned home from the worst day of my life. I definitely was not in the mood to measure Simon.

"My project is a loser." Simon lowered his eyes. "A total loser."

It was hard not to feel sorry for Simon. He was so serious about his science project.

I tried to cheer him up. "Simon, we just don't grow that fast," I said. "Maybe you should study something else. How about measuring a puppy? Puppies grow faster than we do. Much faster."

"But we don't have a puppy," Simon replied.

"How about Brutus? You can measure Brutus," I said, guiding Simon out of my bedroom.

"Brutus isn't going to grow anymore," Simon whined. "You know that. He's too old."

"I'll think about it," I told him. "I'll try to come up with something you can study. But I need to think — alone."

I gave Simon a soft shove out of my room. Then I closed the door.

I flopped down on my bed. And pulled the covers over my head.

I wanted to disappear.

I couldn't face anyone — not Roxanne, not my teacher, not the librarian. Not the whole seventh grade.

I heard a noise.

I whipped off the blanket — and saw my window sliding up. "Phew. Why is it so hot in here?" a familiar voice demanded.

"Oh, noooo," I groaned. "You're back?"

"Lighten up, Sammy. Why don't we go out and play some ball or something? Take your mind off things. I'm a really good pitcher."

"Brent — you have to leave."

"Good idea. Let's leave this stuffy house. We'll go out. Get a pizza. I'm hungry," he said. "You must be hungry too."

"I mean it. You have to go," I said softly. I didn't want to hurt his feelings. I just wanted him to go.

"But I don't want to leave," Brent replied. "I want to be your best friend. I really do."

"I can't be your best friend," I told him. "It's not working out."

"Just give it a chance," he insisted. "We're going to have a great time together. You'll see. . . . "

"Sammy! Time for dinner!" Mom called up the steps.

"I'm going downstairs to eat," I told Brent. "And when I come back —"

"Don't worry, I'll still be here," he said cheerfully.

He's never going to leave, I realized as I headed down for dinner. Never. What am I going to do? How am I going to get rid of him?

There was only one thing to do.

I took my seat at the dinner table. "Mom. Dad. I have something important to tell you."

My parents gazed up from their plates.

I took a deep breath while they waited for me to go on.

"There's an invisible kid in my room — and I need your help. I have to get rid of him!"

I had to tell Mom and Dad.

I didn't know what else to do.

Mom and Dad were really smart — for parents. They were scientists, after all. They'd know how to get rid of Brent.

"Not now, Sammy," Mom said impatiently. "Your father and I had a very hard day today. We worked for hours on the Molecule Detector Light — and it's still not working properly."

She sighed. "After dinner we're going down to the basement to work on it some more. So eat quickly. We don't have time for your wild stories."

I felt a kick under the table. "Cut it out, Simon." I glared at my brother.

"It wasn't me." Simon smirked. "It was the invisible kid!"

Great. Simon, the serious mutant, is trying to be funny.

I kicked Simon back.

"Hey — that hurt!" he whined.

"It wasn't my fault. Your legs are in the way. They must be growing. Quick! Measure them!" I snickered.

"Ha ha." Simon rolled his eyes. "Is the invisible kid as funny as you are?" He kicked me again.

"Simon —" I started.

"Cut it out, you two!" Dad shouted.

I turned to Dad. "But there really is an invisible kid. You've got to believe me. I need your help."

"Not tonight," Dad groaned. "Please. Your mom and I had such a terrible day."

I tried again. "He could be dangerous. He's upstairs and —"

"Sammy — not another word. I mean it," Dad said. "No more crazy stories."

So much for smart parents.

Now what am I going to do? I wondered as Mom

placed our dinner on the table. I've got to get rid of Brent. But how?

All through dinner, I thought and thought. And by the time Mom served dessert, I had an idea!

19

"Brent? Are you here?"

I held out a few pieces of chicken wrapped in a napkin. It was easy sneaking it out of the dining room.

Mom and Dad talked about work all through dinner. Light refraction. Frequency waves. The usual stuff. They didn't pay any attention to me.

And Simon was too busy worrying about his science project. He was still the same size. He even measured his fingernails, but they hadn't grown, either.

When no one was looking, I wrapped the chicken in my napkin and placed it in my lap — and Brutus wailed.

Brutus loves chicken.

He tried to jump into my lap.

He clawed at the napkin.

He wailed some more.

"Can't you do something about that cat?" Mom asked. "Your father and I can't think."

"Come on, Brutus." I shoved the napkin under my T-shirt. "Let's go upstairs."

I jumped up from my chair and waved for Brutus to follow me. He let out a sharp cry — and ran in the other direction.

Wow! Brutus knows! I realized. Brutus knows that something weird is upstairs in my room.

I bet that's why he won't sleep in my room anymore!

I hurried to my room and held out the chicken. "Brent — aren't you hungry?" I stood in one spot. I turned in a circle, holding out the chicken.

"I'm starving. Thanks. Thanks a lot." I felt a light tug as Brent took the food from my hand.

I watched the napkin unfold by itself.

"Mmmm. Fried chicken." A big bite disappeared. "This is excellent. Your mom is a great cook! Thanks."

"Roxanne's mom is a great cook too," I said. "Better than my mom. Much better. I eat at Roxanne's house all the time. Whenever I can."

Brent kept on eating.

"You should eat at Roxanne's. You'd see what I mean."

Brent kept on eating.

"Hey! I just thought of a great idea!" I said. "You should be *Roxanne's* best friend. Roxanne needs a ghost for our school project. You could be the ghost! That would make Roxanne so happy! She would have a ghost right in her own house.

And you'd be happy too — eating all that great food! Come on! I can take you over there right now!"

Brent stopped eating.

"I am *not* going to Roxanne's house," he declared. "She's a girl. I don't want to be a girl's best friend. I want to be your best friend. And I already told you — I am not a ghost."

The empty napkin floated toward me. "Is there any more chicken?" he asked. "I'm still hungry! And how about some dessert?"

I sat down on my bed and waited for Brent to finish his second helping of chicken and the bowl of ice cream I sneaked upstairs for him.

Then I tried again. "Brent, you have to leave. You have to go."

"But I want to be your best friend!" he insisted. "I'm never leaving. NEVER!"

"Don't you get it? I don't *want* you to be my friend," I told him. "I have plenty of friends — at least I did, until you came along."

I stood up and paced back and forth across my room. "You are ruining my life," I said. "I want you to leave. I want you to get out of my house and never come back!"

Silence.

"Do you hear me?"

More silence.

"I know you're here, Brent. Answer me!"

"Please — can we talk later?" he finally replied. "I'm way tired. I need to get some rest."

The covers on my bed began to fold down. Then an invisible hand punched the pillow.

"Ahhhh," Brent sighed. "Your bed is so great!"

That's when I lost it. "We *cannot* talk later. We have to talk now. I want you to get out!" I screamed. "NOW!"

"Really?" Brent's voice changed. Deeper — and meaner. A lot meaner.

"Y-yes. Really," I stammered.

"And what if I won't go?" he asked.

I took a step back — away from the bed.

I didn't like the way Brent said that. It sounded like a threat.

"Well, Sammy — what if I won't go?" he repeated menacingly.

I took another step back — and felt a hot hand clamp down on my shoulder.

I tried to break free — but I couldn't. He was too strong.

Brent grabbed my arm. He held it tightly.

"Leave me alone!" I shouted. "Let me go!"

But he started to pull me — toward the open window!

20

What did he plan to do?

Push me out the window?

"Stop! Let go! Hey — let *go!*" I shot my arms up — and broke free.

"Sorry," Brent muttered. "I was just goofing. You know. Good friends wrestle sometimes — right? Just for fun?"

"Fun?" I cried weakly. My heart pounded in my chest.

He's dangerous, I realized.

I don't think he was kidding around. I think he wanted to shove me out the window.

Frightened, I turned and started to run to the door. But I stumbled over his invisible feet and fell hard to the floor.

Before I could scramble up, I felt his strong hands grab me again.

"*Let go!*" I screeched, my voice high and shrill in panic.

"I was just trying to help you up," Brent said.

His hands released me.

I rubbed my sore wrists.

"Really. I was just helping you up," Brent insisted. "You believe me, don't you? Say you believe me."

"Okay. Okay," I grumbled. "I believe you."

"Great!" Brent cheered.

"But you still have to leave," I told him. "Everyone already thinks I'm too weird. I can't have an invisible boy following me around, talking to me, living in my bedroom. Now go. Really. I mean it."

"But I can help you," Brent cried. "I helped you already — with that math equation."

"Oh, yeah. You helped me all right." I started pacing my room again. "You helped me look like a total geek in front of all my friends — and my teacher." I winced just thinking about it.

"Okay. I made a mistake. One little mistake," Brent said.

"ONE little mistake!" My voice started to rise. "What about in the library today? Now the librarian thinks I'm totally crazy. She wants me to see the guidance counselor!"

I couldn't help myself. I was yelling at him now. "And what about the track race? You ruined everything! You made me fall and lose the race. You made me disappoint everyone."

"Sorry," Brent said softly. "I thought I could help you win. I just wanted to give you a boost."

"A *boost*?" I screamed. "You — you —"

My closet door opened.

My new, dark-blue Yankees baseball jacket floated out. "Hey — cool jacket!" Brent exclaimed. "I think the sleeves are too long, though. I don't think it will fit me."

The jacket slid off the hanger.

"Give that to me!" I snatched the jacket out of the air. "Now — leave! I don't want you here."

"Sammy — who on earth are you yelling at?" Mom stood in my bedroom doorway.

"The invisible kid!" I cried. "He's here! He's right here! You've got to believe me! Brent — say something!"

Silence.

"PLEASE, Brent!" I begged.

Nothing.

Mom walked over to me slowly, staring at me, shaking her head. She placed a hand on my forehead. "You don't seem to have a fever."

"I'm not sick, Mom. I'm fine. Really. And I'm telling the truth."

"I don't know . . ." Her voice trailed off. Then she studied me carefully. "Where are you going?" she asked.

"I'm not going anywhere," I said.

"Then why are you holding your jacket?"

I stared down at the jacket. "Oh, I just wanted to see if it still fits," I lied. I mean — what else could I say now?

"Of course it still fits. We bought it for you last

week." Mom stared hard at me. She placed her hand on my forehead again. "I don't know," she repeated. "You haven't been yourself lately."

She glanced at my jacket again. Then she shook her head some more. "Now tell me — who were you shouting at?"

"Uh . . . no one. I was just rehearsing my lines . . . for the school play."

"You're in the school play?" she asked.

"Uh . . . no. Not exactly," I said. "I'm rehearsing . . . in case they ask me to be in it."

"Sammy, if something is bothering you — you know you can always tell me about it. Right?"

"Right," I said.

Mom felt my forehead for the third time. She shook her head — again. She started for the door — and stopped.

"Your father and I have been working very hard. I know we haven't been paying much attention to you. But that's going to change now. We're going to be here for you. In fact, we're going to be watching you very closely."

Great.

Mom and Dad were going to start studying me — like one of their science projects.

"It's way too chilly in here, Sammy." Mom walked over to my window and closed it. Then she left the room.

"Are you still here, Brent?" I snapped.

"Yes."

"Why did you do that to me? Why wouldn't you speak to my mother?" I demanded.

"Sorry," Brent said. "But I don't want anyone else to know about me. I just want to live with you and be your friend."

"Well, that's not going to happen," I replied sharply.

I suddenly felt hopeful. Because Mom had just given me a great idea!

Now I knew exactly what I had to do — to get rid of the invisible boy.

21

I ran straight across the hall to the bathroom. I turned the hot-water faucet in the shower up all the way.

Yes! A few seconds later, the mirror started to cloud with steam. Then I turned on the hot water in the sink — and in the bathtub too.

Wow. Was it hot in here! Hotter than a tropical rain forest, I thought.

Excellent!

I wiped the sweat from my forehead and raced back into my room. I made sure the window was closed tightly. Then I opened the valve on my radiator. I kept turning it — until I heard the loud hiss of steam escape into my room.

Perspiration dripped from my face as the moist, warm air from the bathroom drifted into my room.

"Sammy, what are you doing?" Brent wailed. "It's too hot in here!"

I laughed. "Sorry. But this is the way I like it!"

I raced down the hall and opened the valve on

Mom and Dad's radiator, then Simon's radiator too. I made sure all their windows were shut tight.

"Sammy, stop!" Brent begged. "It's too hot! Too hot!"

I sat in my bed — and waited.

Beads of sweat formed on my upper lip. My T-shirt, drenched with sweat, clung to me.

Perfect!

"I — I can't take it anymore." Brent's voice started to grow faint. "I — I can't stay here. It's . . . too . . . hot."

Over his low cries, I heard my window slide up.

And I knew that my plan had worked. Brent was gone — for good.

22

On Saturday night, Roxanne and I had planned to go to the movies to see *School Spirit*. But the plan had changed. Roxanne insisted that if I didn't go to Hedge House with her, she'd never speak to me again.

I believed her.

"Can you walk a little faster?" Roxanne asked. "It's getting cold out here."

She was right. A heavy fog had settled in. And a strong wind began to blow.

I shivered in the damp night air.

We walked quickly, down block after block. "We're almost there," Roxanne said as we neared the next corner. "Are you ready?"

I shrugged. "Sure."

"Good." Roxanne stopped. "We're here."

Whoa! I peered up — at the highest, darkest hedges I had ever seen. A wall of hedges so thick you couldn't even see through it!

"I — I've never seen hedges grow so high before," I stammered.

"'It's the will of the ghost. To keep the house chilly and dark — as cold and icy as the spirit itself.'" Roxanne smiled. "I memorized that part from the book I read to you."

"How do we get in?" I asked, searching for a way through the tall shrubs.

"You're lucky you have *me* for a partner," Roxanne sighed. "You don't know anything."

We walked along the dark hedges until we came to a small opening. I peeked inside — and there stood Hedge House. Three stories high, tall and narrow, with lots of windows — most of them shattered. Sharp shards of glass poked up from the frames.

Wow! The hedges did grow as tall as the highest windows — just as the book said. The shingles on the outside of the house were blackened and rotted with age.

A strong gust of wind blew.

The hedge tops beat against the pointed roof — and sent a loose shingle hurtling through the air.

Roxanne and I jumped back — just in time.

I could see Roxanne shiver.

This house was really creepy!

"If you're scared, we don't have to go in," I told her. "We can still go see the movie."

"*Me? Scared?* Have you totally lost it?" she snapped. "Let's go!"

Roxanne headed up the broken stone steps to the front door. I followed right behind her.

She walked up onto the wooden porch. "Be careful," she said, glancing back at me. "These planks are kind of wobbly."

She reached out for the front door. She slowly turned the doorknob.

The door swung open with a creak — and we stepped inside.

23

We stood in a large entrance hall.

A fancy chandelier hung from the ceiling directly over our heads. Crystals in the shape of teardrops dangled from it. Crystals draped in a thick layer of dust and cobwebs.

It felt icy cold in here. Much colder than outside. A sour odor rose up to greet us.

I shivered. I groped for a light switch, and found one on the wall next to the door.

I flicked the switch — but nothing happened.

"It's not going to work!" Roxanne whispered. "Nobody has lived here for years! Turn on your flashlight."

"What flashlight?" I asked.

"You didn't bring a flashlight? You were supposed to bring a flashlight," she whispered.

"I forgot," I admitted.

Roxanne sighed. "Did you bring the camcorder?" she demanded.

"Yes, it's right here." I pulled the video camera out of my backpack.

"At least you remembered *something*," she muttered. She started to say something else. But instead, a cry escaped her lips.

"What's wrong?" I asked.

"Didn't you hear something — like a low moan?" she asked, excited.

"No," I told her. "I didn't hear anything."

"Oh," she said. "Well, we just got here. I bet we hear moaning soon. Make sure your camcorder is ready."

We stepped forward — into the living room. Into a cold white mist.

"I can't see a thing," I whispered. "How did the living room get so foggy?"

"Look." Roxanne pointed to one of the walls where the fog came seeping through the cracks. It entered in narrow streams, then billowed and swirled, filling the room.

I took another step — and the wind howled outside.

Something white flew at me.

I jumped back — then realized it was just the curtains. Filmy, white curtains flapping over the broken front windows. Flapping hard.

Another gust blew. Stronger this time. It drove the streams of fog through the cracks.

"There's nothing in here," I said. Another shiver ran through me. "Let's go upstairs."

Roxanne led the way through the dining room and kitchen before we headed toward the steps. Both rooms were empty. Cold and empty.

We walked down a long hallway. At the end of the hallway we found the staircase. The old, wood banister was badly splintered. Parts of it were missing completely.

"Ready?" Roxanne groped the wall as she started up.

I whispered "yes," but I wasn't so sure. I mean — I really didn't think this house was haunted. But it was so dark, and damp, and foggy, and empty. . . . *Anyone* would be a little scared in here!

As we climbed the staircase, the steps groaned under our feet. The air grew colder.

At the top of the stairs we faced three doors. We peered into each doorway. Into small, dark rooms.

I let out a relieved sigh when I saw they were all empty.

We climbed the stairs to the third floor. It took us into a large room. This one wasn't empty.

Shredded clothing and torn blankets lay scattered on the floor. Three pillows sat propped against a wall — slashed, with the stuffing spilling out.

A toppled wooden chair leaned against an old trunk.

Roxanne crossed the darkened room and headed for the trunk.

I kneeled down and studied a piece of black, crumpled material on the floor. I picked it up — and gasped.

It was a black shirt — a black shirt with the right sleeve missing! Just like in the ghost story!

"Let's check out the trunk," Roxanne whispered.

"No! Look at this —" I started, then stopped — as a frightening moan drifted up the steps.

We spun around to face the staircase — and gasped as the steps began to creak and groan.

Footsteps!

Roxanne's mouth gaped open.

My heart began to pound in my chest.

Roxanne turned to me, but I peered down quickly so she wouldn't see how frightened I was.

"The — the ghost — is here," she stammered. "It's coming! Get the camcorder ready."

I fumbled for the power switch. It shook as I raised it up in my trembling hands.

The footsteps reached the top of the stairs.

Roxanne stood in the center of the room — frozen in fear.

A deep, eerie moan filled the room. Followed by a shrill laugh.

Then the chair flew across the room. And the lid of the trunk shot open.

Roxanne leaped back. She took out her notebook and began scribbling notes. She was excited — and scared. Her pencil shook as she wrote.

The lid of the trunk slammed down hard. We both jumped.

I watched in horror as the chair began to rise up off the floor. It hovered in midair, then came down with a loud crash.

"Don't just stand there!" Roxanne screamed at me. "The camcorder! The camcorder! Get it on video!"

I lifted the video camera — and the pillows soared through the room.

The blankets came alive. They seemed to hurl themselves at us. They wrapped around our bodies.

"Yuck!" I cried out. They smelled so sour, so rotten.

The blankets spun us around like toy tops. Then they dropped to the floor.

The trunk lid opened and banged closed — again and again.

The windows slid up and crashed down.

"It's a ghost!" Roxanne exclaimed happily. "A real ghost! Do you believe it? We're definitely going to get an A! Let me have that!"

She grabbed my video camera. And peered through the viewfinder.

"Noooooooo!" A terrified howl escaped her throat. She dropped the camera. It clattered to the floor.

"Help me, Sammy!" she screamed. "It's got me! It's got me!"

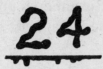

24

"Let me go!" Roxanne shrieked. "Sammy — help! It's got me! The ghost — it's *pulling* me!"

I gaped in horror as Roxanne's jacket flew up behind her, tugged by an invisible, ghostly hand.

Her whole body jerked as the ghost pulled — and sent her stumbling across the room.

She tripped and fell to her knees.

"Owww!" She uttered a terrified cry. Scrambled to her feet, her eyes wide with fright.

I suddenly remembered the camcorder. I've *got* to get this on tape! I told myself. I raised the camera.

Roxanne's jacket flew out behind her again. "Ohhh — help!" she cried.

She began to spin in a circle. Round and round. Faster and faster. Whirling helplessly, her arms flying up, her hair spinning out behind her head.

I tried to hold the camcorder steady, but I couldn't.

"Drop that stupid camera — and help me!" Roxanne shrieked as she whirled around the room.

"Get away from her!" I yelled. "Leave her alone!"

To my shock, Roxanne stopped spinning. Her knees buckled. She fell against the wall. Hit hard with a loud *THUD*.

"Oh." She shook her head as if trying to shake away her fear. "The Ghost of Hedge House —" she started.

But before she could finish her sentence, she floated up from the floor.

"No — please!" Roxanne begged, thrashing her arms wildly; kicking her legs. "LET ME DOWN! LET ME DOWN!"

The ghost must have let go. Because Roxanne slid to the floor. She landed on her knees.

Before she could climb up, a pillow floated from the floor. I stared in shock as it pressed itself over Roxanne's face.

She uttered a muffled cry. "Help — I can't breathe! The ghost — he's *smothering* me!"

"Nooooo!" A cry tore from my throat as I dove across the room to Roxanne.

"Nooooo!" With a desperate grab, I ripped the pillow away. "Go haunt someone else!" I screamed.

Roxanne dropped to the floor.

I tossed the pillow away and started toward her. But a cold hand tightened around my arm. "*Jeffrey — I've been waiting for you,*" a hoarse voice rasped.

The Ghost of Hedge House!

It talked! It talked to *me*!

"I — I'm not Jeffrey!" I choked out.

"*Jef-frey — I've been waiting for you!*" he moaned again.

Then I felt myself being lifted off the floor.

Before I could struggle free, the ghost jerked me back and forth — back and forth — so hard I thought my neck would snap.

I wanted to scream. I wanted to fight back.

But his grip was so strong. I felt so helpless. . . .

A sour-smelling blanket rose up and wrapped itself tightly around me. I couldn't move my hands or legs!

I kicked and squirmed — struggling against the rotted fabric. And finally dropped facedown on the floor.

A shrill laugh rang through the room.

Roxanne and I staggered to our feet. We headed for the stairs.

The ghost followed after us, moaning. "*Jeffrey — I've been waiting for you. Jeffrey — come back! I've waited so long!*"

We reached the second-floor landing — and the ghost grabbed me from behind. "*I've got you now,*

Jef-frey!" came his raspy whisper. *"I've waited so long in this old house. So long . . . "*

His cold hands circled my neck.

He tightened his grip. I couldn't breathe!

"I'm . . . not . . . Jeffrey," I choked out.

My last words.

25

I thought they were my last words.

Everything flared bright red. The dark room spun and tilted behind the swirling red.

Stars flashed in my eyes. So white and bright, my head ached. I tried to blink them away.

And they faded to black. Everything faded to black.

The Ghost of Hedge House had another victim.

But no.

Not quite.

A hand grabbed mine. Pulled me. Pulled me from the darkness.

"Sammy — come on!" Roxanne pleaded in a terrified whisper. "Come on! You're okay! You're okay!"

And before I realized it, she had pulled me free. And we were running again. Running down the stairs. Through the misty living room. Out the door. And into the cold night.

Breathing the air. The cool, sweet air.

Breathing and running.

Alive!

Yes! Alive! Leaving the Ghost of Hedge House behind. And running. Running and breathing.

The air never smelled so good. The night never looked so beautiful.

Roxanne ran straight to her house. I watched her throw open her front door. She flew inside and slammed the door behind her.

I jogged the rest of the way to my house. Burst breathlessly inside. And checked the front door twice to make sure it was locked.

My legs trembling, my whole body vibrating, shaking — *alive!* — I ran up the stairs to my room.

I sat down on my bed — and screamed in terror. Screamed at the black shirt draped on my pillow.

The black shirt of the one-armed ghost!

26

"It's only a shirt," a voice said calmly. "What's your problem?"

I jumped to my feet — and saw a plate hovering in the air. And a sandwich vanishing, bite by bite.

Brent!

"Didn't I do a great job?" Brent asked between bites. "Don't I make an awesome ghost?"

I saw my desk chair slide out. "That was hard work!" he sighed. "Boy, am I tired!"

"You?" I shrieked. "That was *you*?"

"I know. I know. I was awesome," he said. *"Jef-frey — I've been waiting for you!"* Then he burst out laughing.

"I — I — I —" I sputtered.

"Don't thank me," Brent said. "Really. You don't have to thank me. Now you'll have the best report in school. I told you I could help you. I told you I could be your best friend."

"Oh, nooo!" I shouted. "Brent! How could you do that to me? You scared me to death! You scared

Roxanne to death! You really hurt her! And you nearly strangled me!"

"Don't thank me," he repeated. "You really don't have to. I just wanted to show that I can help you."

"Get out of my house! Get out — *now!*" I screamed at him. "I mean it!"

"GET OUT!" I cried, so loud my voice cracked. "Get out, you idiot! You nearly killed us! I want you to leave NOW. Get out!"

I turned to the door and pointed to it. "Get —"

Dad stood in the doorway, his face filled with concern. "Sammy, I'm sorry, son. But you're too old to have an imaginary friend," he said softly.

"No, Dad. You don't understand! He's not my friend!" I cried. "He's not my friend! He's not!"

Dad wrapped his arm around my shoulders. "Stay calm. Just try to stay calm."

He walked me to my bed. He made me sit down. He grabbed for my desk chair.

"Don't sit there!" I gasped. "*He's* sitting there!"

Dad sat down anyway. "Take a deep breath," he instructed me. "Settle down. Now — let's talk about this friend of yours."

"Dad! He's not my friend. He wants to be my friend, but he's not. He's driving me crazy!"

I shoved the black shirt aside and fell back on my pillow. And suddenly I had an idea. "I know! I bet we can get rid of him together! Dad — will you help me? Will you help me get rid of Brent?"

"Of course I'll help you," Dad replied, his eyes studying me. He stood up. Took my hand. Guided me to the doorway.

"Thanks, Dad! I really appreciate this. Thanks a lot." I sighed with relief.

I suddenly felt much better. As soon as Dad said he'd help, all my muscles relaxed.

"Everything is going to be okay," Dad said softly.

"I know," I replied. "I feel better already."

"That's great, son. But can you tell me — what's troubling you? Do you know? What made you invent this invisible friend — Brent?"

I let out a loud groan.

Dad didn't believe me. He led me downstairs.

"Where are we going?" I asked.

He didn't answer me.

"Dad!" I cried. "*Where* are you taking me?"

27

"Where are we going, Dad? TELL ME NOW!"

"Calm down, Sammy. We have an appointment with someone who can help you," he finally answered. "Mom and I have talked about your problem with Dr. Krandall — and she's going to see you now."

"I — I don't want to go to a doctor!" I yelled. "I don't need a doctor!"

"Don't worry." Dad patted me on the back. "You'll like talking to the doctor. She's really nice. And very understanding."

Dad hurried to the kitchen to get his car keys.

Dad thinks I'm crazy, I realized. He thinks I've totally lost it.

So does everyone else I know.

There's no way I can convince anyone that Brent is real.

He's going to live with me forever.

He's going to ruin my life forever.

Someone knocked at the door. I pulled it open.

"Hi, Sammy." It was Roxanne. "I had to come over!" she said. "I *had* to talk to you about the ghost! Wasn't that awesome?"

"Uh-huh. Really awesome," I murmured.

"Well, you don't sound very excited. What's the matter with you?" She headed into the living room and sat down on the couch.

"Oh, nothing. Everyone thinks I'm crazy — that's all." I sat down beside her.

Brutus sauntered in and curled up in my lap.

"Did you tell your parents about the ghost? Is that why they think you're crazy? Don't worry! I'll tell them it's all true," Roxanne assured me. "I'll tell them we really saw it!"

"It's not about the ghost —"

"Okay, Sammy. Let's go." Dad walked into the room, jingling the car keys in his hand.

Mom and Simon followed behind him, both wearing very serious expressions.

"Where are you going?" Roxanne asked. "Can I come too?"

"No, Roxanne. I don't think that would be a good idea," Dad said softly. "I'm taking Sammy to a doctor. He's been seeing things."

"But everything is going to be okay," Mom chimed in. She gazed at me with a strange smile on her face. "Doctors know how to deal with these things."

"You don't have to take Sammy to a doctor," Roxanne started. "The ghost —"

"Is your invisible friend a ghost? You didn't tell me that part," Mom said.

"Your invisible friend?" Roxanne's eyebrows shot up. "He's still in your room?"

"Wait, Dad — don't take Sammy to the doctor!" Simon exclaimed.

Whoa. I couldn't believe this one. Simon was actually sticking up for me.

"Don't take him tonight," Simon added. "Take him tomorrow. He'll still be crazy tomorrow. I want you to help me with my science project tonight. I'm not growing fast enough. I want you to help me come up with a new topic."

"It will have to wait, Simon. Your brother needs help," Dad said sternly. "Come on, Sammy. Let's go."

"I am *not* going to a doctor!" I shouted. "Wait. What if I *prove* that Brent is real?"

I didn't give them a chance to answer. I had a plan. A really good plan. If it worked, they'd believe me. They'd *have* to believe me.

I charged down to the basement. And searched Dad's workbench.

Where is it? Where is it? I searched frantically. *It's got to be here somewhere!*

I cleared the benchtop with a swipe of my hand. Everything clattered to the floor. But I found it!

The Molecule Detector Light.

I charged back upstairs. "This light lets you see invisible things, right?" I waved the light in Dad's

108

face. "So if I shine it on Brent, we'll all be able to see him! Right, Dad? Right?"

"Maybe," Dad replied doubtfully. "But, Sammy —"

I ran to the stairs. Everyone followed me.

Will it work? I wondered. Will it?

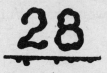

28

"Where are you, Brent? I know you're here."

Everyone crowded into my room.

They watched me as I slowly turned in a circle, searching for a clue. Searching for something that would tell me where Brent was.

"Brent!" I called his name.

He didn't answer me.

I turned on the detector light.

I swept it through the room.

No sign of Brent anywhere.

"Sammy, this is silly," Mom said. She turned to Dad for support, but Dad just shrugged his shoulders.

I kneeled down and swept the light under my bed.

No Brent.

"Please put the light down," Mom pleaded. "We're wasting time. We have an appointment with the doctor."

I ignored her.

"Where are you, Brent? I know you're here!" I said. "Tell us where you are — now!"

And then, finally, Brent spoke up. "Please. Please don't do it, Sammy. Please — I don't want you to see me."

Mom, Dad, Simon, and Roxanne gasped.

"See!" I cried. "I told you! I told you he was here! I told you I'm not crazy!"

I swept the light over my desk chair. Onto my bed. In front of my dresser. But Brent wasn't any of those places.

"Where are you, Brent? It's okay. You can tell me. I have to show them."

"Please. NO!" Brent cried. "I don't want you to!"

I jerked open the closet door.

I shined the light inside — and I saw him!

"NO! I don't believe it!" I gasped. "You're — you're a MONSTER!"

29

"You're a MONSTER!" I cried again.

The Molecule Detector Light shook in my trembling hand. I forced myself to hold the bright beam steady.

"That's why my parents made me invisible," Brent said softly. "They thought I might survive if you couldn't see me."

With my light still focused on him, Brent stepped toward me.

I leaped back. "What are you going to do?"

"Whoa — he is so UGLY!" Simon groaned. "Yuck! He has only *one* head!"

"And look. He has only two arms — and they're so short!" Roxanne cried. "He can't wrap his arms around and around himself. How does he keep himself warm?"

"And what's that dark stuff growing on top of his head?" Simon pointed. "Why doesn't he have tendrils and suction pods like we do? Where are his antennae? And how can he see with only *two* eyes?"

"Calm down, everyone," Dad instructed. "You're not going to harm us — are you, Brent?"

"No. Of course not," Brent replied. "I just want to be Sammy's friend."

"No! Be *my* friend!" Simon cried. "I need you for my science project!"

Simon turned to Dad. "Can I have him, Dad? PLEASE! Can I have him for my science project? I really need him!"

"That wouldn't be fair," Roxanne replied. "Sammy found him first!"

"Everyone — quiet!" Mom ordered. "Brent — I've seen pictures of your species in a textbook. Hmm . . . let me see . . . what are you called?"

"I'm called a human," Brent answered shyly.

"That's right!" Mom snapped her fingers. "Now I remember. Human."

"Yuck," Roxanne muttered, making a disgusted face.

"I know I'm ugly," Brent said sadly. "That's why I didn't want you to see me . . . " His voice trailed off.

I stared at Brent in disbelief. A human. I'd never heard of one before.

I tore my five eyes away from him and turned to Dad. "I know he's ugly, Dad. But I think I'd like to keep him," I said. "Can I? I'll take good care of him. I promise!"

"No. I don't think so, Sammy." Dad studied

Brent for a moment. "I think we'd better take Brent to the zoo."

"Huh? The zoo?" I cried. "Why, Dad? Why does he have to live in a zoo?"

"Well, he'll get much better care there," Dad answered. "After all, humans are an endangered species!"

A few days ago, a new girl started at our school. Her name is Iris Candler. She walked into my class and stood awkwardly at the front of the room, waiting for Ms. Williamson to assign her a seat.

I was busy trying to do the math homework assignment before the bell rang. Somehow I forgot all about it the night before.

I took a few seconds from my furious scribbling to check out the new girl. Kind of cute, I thought. She had a round face with big blue eyes and short blond hair parted in the middle. She wore long, red plastic earrings that jangled when she moved her head.

Ms. Williamson gave Iris a seat near the back. Then she asked me to show Iris around the school during the day. You know. Point out where the lunchroom is and all the bathrooms and everything.

I nearly cried out in surprise. Why did Ms.

Williamson pick me? I guess it was because Iris just happened to be sitting right next to me.

I heard a couple of kids laugh. And I heard someone mutter, "Sicky Ricky."

Kids in my class are always on my case. I hoped that Iris didn't hear them.

I admit it. I wanted to impress her. I liked having someone new to talk to, someone who didn't know that everyone thought I was a loser.

At lunchtime I walked Iris downstairs to the lunchroom. I told her about how new the school was. And how when we moved in for the first time, hot water came out of all the cold water faucets, and cold water came out of the hot.

She thought that was pretty funny. I liked the way her earrings jangled when she laughed.

She asked me if I was on any sports teams.

"Not yet," I answered.

Not in a million years! I thought.

Whenever guys are choosing up teams on the playground, the captains always fight over who gets me. It's always:

"*You* take him!"

"No fair! *You* have to take him!"

"No. *You* take him! We had him last time!"

I'm not exactly a super jock.

"This is the lunchroom," I told Iris, leading the way through the door. I instantly felt really dumb. I mean, what *else* could it be? The band room?

As soon as I entered, I saw my four enemies at their usual table in the middle of the room. I call them my four enemies because . . . they're my four enemies!

Their names are Jared, David, Brenda, and Wart. Wart's name is really Richard Wartman. But everyone calls him Wart — even the teachers.

These four seventh-graders are always making fun of me. When they're not making fun of me, they're trying to *injure* me!

I don't know what their problem is. I never did anything to them. I guess they pick on me because I'm easy to pick on.

I grabbed two food trays and guided Iris to the food counter. "This is hot food over here," I explained. "No one ever eats the hot food unless it's pizza or hamburgers."

Iris flashed me a nice smile. "Just like at my old school," she said.

"Be sure to stay away from the macaroni," I warned. "No one ever eats the macaroni. We think they serve the same macaroni all year. See that crust on top? Whoever heard of macaroni with a crust?"

Iris laughed. I brushed back my hair. I wondered if she liked me.

We both picked up sandwiches and bags of potato chips. I put a bowl of red and green Jell-O and a bottle of kiwi-strawberry drink on my tray. "The cashier is over here," I told Iris.

I showed Iris how you hand your food ticket to the cashier and get it punched. I was feeling pretty good. I think Iris was impressed by all my helpful instructions.

I spotted a couple of seats at a table near the window. I motioned to them with my head. Then I started through the crowded, noisy room, holding my tray high in both hands.

Of course I didn't see Wart stick his foot out.

I tripped over it. Fell forward. And my whole tray went flying.

I hit the floor in time to look up and see the red and green Jell-O bound across a table and onto a girl's lap. The rest of my food slid over the floor.

Kids laughed and cheered and clapped.

"There goes Ricky!" someone exclaimed. "Ricky Rat! Ricky Rat!"

Wart and his three pals started chanting: "Sicky Ricky . . . Sicky Ricky!"

I glanced up and saw Iris laughing too.

I just wanted to disappear.

My face suddenly felt burning hot. I knew I was blushing.

What am I going to do? I thought, lying there on my stomach. *I really can't take this any longer.*

What can I do?

After school I made my way to the eighth-grade classrooms at the end of the building. The school newspaper office is in Ms. Richards's room.

Ms. Richards sat at her desk, grading papers. As I stepped into the doorway, she glanced up and frowned. Then she returned to her work.

I saw Tasha typing furiously at the computer in the corner. Her lips moved as she wrote. Her forehead furrowed in heavy concentration.

I walked over to the assistant editor, an eighth-grader named Melly. Melly has short, straight brown hair and wears glasses with brown frames that match her hair. She was leaning over a long news story, running her finger down the page as she read.

"Hi, Melly," I said.

She glanced up and frowned too. "Ricky — you made me lose my place."

"Sorry," I said. "Any stories for me today?"

You probably wonder why I signed up to be a

reporter on the *Harding Herald*. It's not that I'm a great writer or anything.

Every kid at Harding needs twenty activity points a year. That means you have to try out for sports or join clubs or other after-school activities.

No way I was going to try out for a sport. So I signed up for the newspaper. I thought it would be easy.

That's because I hadn't met Tasha yet.

Tasha treats all sixth-graders like bugs. She makes a disgusted face when a sixth-grader walks into the room. Then she tries to step on us.

She gives all the good story assignments to eighth-graders. Do you know the first story she asked me to write? She asked me to count the dirt patches in the playground and write about why grass didn't grow there.

I knew she was just trying to get me out of the office. But I wrote the story anyway. It's hard to write a good story about dirt patches. But I did a really good job. My story was five pages long!

She never printed it in the paper.

When I asked her why, she said, "Who cares about dirt patches?"

My next assignment was to interview the night janitor about the differences between working days and nights.

That one didn't get into the paper, either.

I wanted to quit. But I really needed the activity

points. If I didn't earn twenty activity points, I couldn't graduate from sixth grade. I'd have to go to summer school. Really.

So I kept coming to the *Harding Herald* office two or three afternoons a week after school, asking Tasha for more news stories to write.

"Anything for me?" I asked Melly.

She shrugged. "I don't know. Ask Tasha."

I moved over to Tasha's desk. Her face reflected the blue monitor as she typed away. "Any stories for me?" I asked her.

She kept typing. She didn't glance up. "Wait till I'm finished," she snarled.

I backed away. I turned and saw Ms. Richards walk out of the room. Some kids were talking by the table near the window, so I crossed over to them.

David and Wart — two of my enemies — were arguing about something. They're both sports reporters for the paper. They write about all the Harding games. The rest of the time they hang around the office, making trouble.

David is tall and blond. Wart is short and lumpy and red-faced. He looks a little like a wart!

I saw some cookies and cans of soda on the table. I tried to walk around David and Wart to get to the drinks. But Wart stepped in front of me.

He and David both grinned. "How was your lunch, Ricky?" Wart asked.

They laughed and slapped each other a high five.

I glared at Wart. I wanted to wipe the grin off his face. "Why did you trip me?" I could feel my face growing hot.

"I didn't," he lied.

David laughed.

"You did too!" I insisted. "You stuck out your foot —"

"No way," he said. "I didn't touch you."

"You tripped over a crack in the floor," David chimed in. "Or maybe it was an air pocket."

They both laughed.

They're so lame.

I grabbed a can of Pepsi off the table, popped it open, and started to walk away.

"Hey, wait —" Wart held me by the shoulder.

I spun around. "What's your problem?"

"That's the can I wanted," he said.

"Too bad. Get your own," I told him.

"No. I want that one." He swiped at the can.

I swung my hand out of his reach.

Lost my grip. And the can went flying across the room.

It sprayed Pepsi as it flew. Then landed in the middle of Tasha's keyboard.

She let out a squeal. Jumped up. Knocked her chair over.

I quickly grabbed up a handful of paper napkins from the table and darted across the room.

"Don't worry. I'll clean it up!" I told Tasha.

The keyboard was soaked. I frantically started to mop the keys.

"No — Ricky — *stop!*" Tasha shrieked.

Too late.

I stared in horror at what I had done.

"Aaaaiiiiii!" Tasha opened her mouth in an angry scream. She tugged at her red hair with both hands.

"You creep! Ricky, you creep!" she cried.

She shouldn't call people names. But she had good reason to be angry at me.

I had erased the whole front page.

The screen glowed at us. Bright blue. Solid blue.

No words. No pictures.

"Uh . . . sorry," I murmured.

"Maybe I can get it back," Tasha told Melly. "Maybe there is a way to find it and pull it back up."

Tasha shoved me out of the way, picked up her chair, and sat down. "Oh!" She let out another cry when she realized she had sat in a puddle of soda.

Staring at the solid blue screen, she began typing furiously.

I could see that the keys were still wet and

sticky. She kept making mistakes. Backing up. Typing again. Typing. Typing. Muttering under her breath the whole time.

No use. No good.

The front page refused to come back.

Finally, she gave up with a loud groan. She tossed her hair in the air with both hands. And turned to me with a growl.

"You creep!" she cried. "All that work! All that work — lost!"

I swallowed hard. "Tasha, it was an accident," I muttered. "Really. It was just an accident."

"You little creep!" Tasha shrieked. Melly stood beside her, glaring at me angrily, shaking her head.

"Wart pushed me!" I cried. I turned to the table. Wart and David had vanished from the room.

"You're off the paper!" Tasha screamed. "Get out, Ricky. You're out of here!"

"Huh?" My heart stopped for a second. "No, Tasha — wait!" I pleaded.

"Get out! Get out!" She made shooing motions with both hands. The way you shoo away a dog. "You're off the paper! I mean it!"

"But — but — but —" I sputtered like an outboard motor. "But I need the activity points! Please give me a second chance! *Please*!" I begged.

"Out!" Tasha insisted.

Melly tsk-tsked and shook her head.

"You're so *unfair!*" I wailed.

I know, I know. I sounded like a baby. But, give me a break. It really *was* unfair.

I turned and slunk to the door. And guess who was standing there. Guess who had watched the whole ugly scene.

You're right.

Iris.

Her first day of school. And she already knew what a loser I was.

"What are *you* doing here?" I asked glumly.

"They said I needed an after-school activity. So I thought I'd try the newspaper," Iris replied. She followed me down the empty hall. "But I don't think I want to join the newspaper. That red-haired girl is really mean."

"Tell me about it," I muttered, rolling my eyes.

"She shouldn't have called you a creep," Iris continued. "It was just an accident. She's horrible! She should give you another chance."

Maybe Iris and I *will* become good friends, I thought.

I pulled my blue parka from my locker. Then Iris and I made our way out of the building.

The afternoon sun was already dropping behind the houses and bare trees. It gets dark so early here in the winter. Patches of snow on the lawns and sidewalk gleamed dully as we walked toward the street.

"Which way is your house?" I asked, shifting my backpack over my parka.

Iris pointed.

"Mine too," I said. We started walking together. I didn't really feel like talking. I was still totally upset about getting kicked off the newspaper.

But I felt glad that Iris was on my side.

We crossed the street and made our way up the next block. A tall hedge stretched along the entire block, broken only by driveways.

Some kids had marked off the street for a street hockey game. They were skating back and forth, leaning on their sticks, cheering and shouting.

"Do you skate?" Iris asked.

"A little," I told her. "My Rollerblades are kind of broken. The brakes came loose and —"

"I always take off the brakes," she said. "It's a lot more fun without the brakes — don't you think?"

I started to answer. But a sound from behind the tall hedge made me stop.

Was someone whispering?

Did I hear someone giggling?

Iris and I kept walking. She was telling me something about how kids skated in the town she moved from. I didn't really listen.

I kept hearing footsteps. Whispers. Scraping sounds. From the other side of the hedge.

Finally, I raised a finger to my lips. "Iris — shhh," I whispered.

Her blue eyes widened in surprise. "Ricky — what's the matter?"

"I think we're being followed," I told her.

"I don't hear anything," Iris whispered. She narrowed her eyes at me.

We both listened.

Silence. Except for the cheers of the street hockey players behind us down the block.

We started walking.

I heard a giggle. Some whispers.

I turned into the next driveway and darted behind the hedge.

"Who's there?" Iris called. She came running up behind me. Her eyes searched the hedge, then the front yard.

"No one here," I said.

She laughed, "Ricky, why do you look so worried? You probably heard a bird or something."

"Yeah. A bird," I repeated. I led the way around the hedge to the sidewalk. I didn't want Iris to think I was crazy. But I knew I'd heard something.

We walked past a few more houses. Then I

heard a whispered chant from behind the hedge: "Sicky Ricky . . . Sicky Ricky . . ."

"Did you hear that?" I asked Iris.

She shook her head. I heard the distant hum of a plane, high overhead. "Do you mean that plane?" she asked.

"No," I replied. "I heard a voice."

A soft giggle floated out from the hedge.

I ran to check it out. Nearly slipped on a slick patch of ice.

I grabbed the hedge to catch my balance. No one back there. An empty front yard.

Straightening my backpack, I hurried to Iris on the sidewalk.

"Ricky, you're a little weird," she said. She laughed. But I could tell she was starting to wonder about me. Starting to think maybe I was too weird to be her friend.

"I heard someone back there. Really," I insisted. "They must be hiding in the hedge or —"

"AAAAAIIIIIII!" I heard a scream of attack!

The hedge shook.

I staggered backwards toward the street.

And four figures came leaping out of the hedge. Four kids shrieking and cheering.

My four enemies!

I saw Iris's face twist in surprise. And then Wart grabbed me. David grabbed me too. Brenda and Jared joined them.

They pushed me one way. Then pulled me back.

Laughing and shouting, they spun me around. Then David tackled me to the ground.

They swarmed around me. Pushed me down. Held me in the cold, wet mud.

"Let go of me!" I shrieked.

I tried to kick and thrash and squirm free. But the four of them held me firmly.

"Let go of me!" I wailed. "What are you going to do?"

About the Author

R.L. Stine's books are read all over the world. So far, his books have sold more than 300 million copies, making him one of the most popular children's authors in history. Besides Goosebumps, R.L. Stine has written the teen series Fear Street, the funny series Rotten School, as well as the Mostly Ghostly series, The Nightmare Room series, and the two-book thriller *Dangerous Girls*. R.L. Stine lives in New York with his wife, Jane, and Minnie, his King Charles spaniel. You can learn more about him at www.RLStine.com.

HE SCARIEST PLACE ON EARTH!

AN ALL-NEW, ALL-TERRIFYING SERIES FROM THE MASTER OF FRIGHT!

Goosebumps HorrorLand

REVENGE OF THE LIVING DUMMY
R.L. STINE
SCHOLASTIC

AN ALL-NEW, ALL-TERRIFYING SERIES FROM THE MASTER OF FRIGHT!

Goosebumps HorrorLand

CREEP FROM THE DEEP
R.L. STINE
SCHOLASTIC

AN ALL-NEW, ALL-TERRIFYING SERIES FROM THE MASTER OF FRIGHT!

Goosebumps HorrorLand

MONSTER BLOOD FOR BREAKFAST!
R.L. STINE
SCHOLASTIC

AN ALL-NEW, ALL-TERRIFYING SERIES FROM THE MASTER OF FRIGHT!

Goosebumps HorrorLand

August 2008!

THE SCREAM OF THE HAUNTED MASK
R.L. STINE
SCHOLASTIC

EnterHorrorLand.com

SCHOLASTIC

The Original Bone-Chilling Serie

Now with All-New Behind-the-Screams
Author Interviews and More!

SCHOLASTIC